The Dhamira Curio and Gift Shop

David T. Boyd

TM

PUBLISHED BY:
ANOTHER SHORE PRESS, LLC
PO BOX 350143
BROOKLYN, NEW YORK 11235
WWW.ANOTHERSHOREPRESS.COM
COVER DESIGN: IVAN CELIN – WWW.IVANCELINCREATIVE.COM

ISBN: 978-0-9832484-6-0

PRINTED IN THE UNITED STATES OF AMERICA

DEDICATION

To Pops, my inspiration.

Volume One: *the death of a salesman*

1: *the stories*

"Balloons"

"Clowns"

"Candles"

"DVDs"

2: *the obituaries*

The Chicago Daily Reader

The Crosstown Herald

3: *the tributes*

"Dear Tommy"

"My Friend, My Brother"

1: *the stories*

BALLOONS

May 19 – 6:10pm

So there I was - standing with several long, thin strings that covered my entire body like a fisherman's net. Spread around me was blown bits of rubber in a variety of colors: red, white, blue, orange, green and even pink. The tied ends of these vibrant colors that managed to hang on for dear life had now dangled around my eyes and ears like the locks of a teenage punk rocker; the helium that filled my chest caused a momentary high, temporarily removing me from the situation I was now in. Too bad that sense of 'uplift' could not have lasted longer, for in addition to the scene I had just described, there stood about forty or so people in my front room – men, women and children, all of whom had come bearing gifts to celebrate my daughter's birthday, but had witnessed something far more ominous than they had originally bargained for.

Even as I describe these events to you, I myself can hardly grasp what had just occurred, but without a doubt I was to pay a heavy price in the very near future for my recent actions, all of which have caused irreversible harm to the lives of my most prized loved ones –

my wife Isabella, and my beautiful daughter Desiree, now ten years old. Though the room was full, it was so quiet that one could hear a feather drop on my tightly looped, beige-colored carpet. Some stared at me with disgust, others tried to calm their children; but what was far more disturbing to me was the look of embarrassment on the face of my daughter who, until now, considered her daddy way above the ranks of 'bestest' of all superheroes, as she would often say. Usually a vibrant, gregarious young lady, she couldn't bear to look at me for what I had done. That, plus the fact I had successfully ruined her tenth birthday, would be enough to make for hundreds of thousands of apologies for many years to come.

"Get out of this house right now, Raymond!" my wife growled, breaking the silence.

I took a deep breath and stepped through the strings, kicking them from my shoes as I made my way toward the front door, leaving behind a perfect circle of shredded balloons – the same ones that had haunted me for three long hours on this horrible day. As I left the house I heard a crisp slap, followed by several people begging Elijah Walker, my now former best friend, to 'please release her'. In this case, the 'her' was more than likely Elijah's wife, Juliana, who had turned out to be my willing accomplice in this oldest and most basic of crimes against any marriage.

For nearly three years I've been having an affair with Juliana. Once, with my wife nearby, I met her in my garage and made love across the hood of my Black 1977 Chevy Corvette – the same one that Isabella bought me for our eleventh year anniversary a few years back. You see, after Desiree was born my wife would hardly touch me anymore. As a psychiatrist, I've long understood the port-traumatic stress some women experience after a difficult pregnancy; I've counseled many young couples who have gone through the exact same thing I am. And though I still loved her, I couldn't live a life without physical intimacy. I wanted desperately to make love to my wife, but I grew tired of being turned away, leaving me frustrated as all hell. Juliana, I found out one day, was regularly abused by Elijah – both physically and mentally. Because she also feared her husband, plus her own lack of financial independence, she had no choice but to remain with him for now. She confessed all of this to me in my office late one evening. For years I had always felt a certain attraction to her, one I was unable to describe. She was pretty, but not beautiful. She was smart, but not someone I would consider scholarly. And despite these facts, for years my heart always skipped a beat whenever she was in my presence. Her confession proved to be the beginning of a torrid love affair as I threw everything from my desk to the floor, shamefully tore off her brand new dress and gave what both of us had wanted for so long. Each other.

But now that was all over; we had finally been caught, and it was my fault.

As I headed toward +my car, I could hear Juliana's cries, followed by a shouting Elijah, as he chased her to their home a few doors down, leaving behind their daughter Chelsea, who had come over to help celebrate Desiree's special day. I thought for certain he would beat the shit out of me, and if he had I would've allowed him to, for I deserved every bit of it. Instead, he would viciously take out his anger out on Juliana. I thought of going over to her house and taking her with me, and I really should have, but I was too much of a coward. All I wanted to do was curl up in a ball and hideaway in some dark corner for the rest of my life. There was no doubt; I had screwed up, and as much as I wanted to, there was no turning back. I was stuck, and it was all because of that store, the weird merchant who ran the place and those balloons.

Those goddamn fucking balloons!

***

May 5 – 12:48pm

All of this began a few weeks prior when I was out doing some shopping for Desiree's birthday with Juliana. We went downtown and bought her several pairs of Sean Jean Jeans, a brand new iPod Nano and two passes to some "A-Teens" (or something like that) concert, which was playing over at the Arie Crown Theater next month. Juliana offered to buy the tickets since Chelsea was also a fan and more than likely would be the one to go with Desiree, but I insisted – being fully aware that she probably couldn't afford it. Poor Julie! Her husband was a successful attorney with a thriving law practice, making over a quarter-million dollars a year, but Elijah was incredibly stingy with everyone, especially with his own. What a despicable human being he was! He had such a wonderful family and lived in one of Northbrook's finest homes, yet refused to treat them with any semblance of decency. Until I found out about his personal life, which he kept tightly wrapped from everyone, I was indeed his friend. We spent long hours drinking at Jo-Jo's Bar and Grille in Bridgeport, split seasons tickets to Bears and White Sox games and joined a neighborhood softball team together. After

Juliana shared with me his personal issues I still did those things with him, but only to throw off any possibility of him suspecting me. It worked out well. As cruel of a man as Elijah was, it never dawned on him that Juliana might play around.

Isabella and I agreed that she would keep Desiree and Chelsea under wraps while I completed the shopping for her party, which was fine with me because I could spend time with Juliana on my own. We hurriedly got through the stores so we could have some play time later, and as I was about to head home, she reminded me that we had one more stop to make; we had to place an order for party favors, ice cream and cake. As I'm sure you can understand by now, my body ached for her in the worst way, so I wanted to get this over with quick. There was one place on the far side of town that I'd used before, but it would take way too much time to get home from there, given the heavy traffic that surely would meet us on the way back. As we drove along South Michigan Avenue I happened to see a small storefront nestled in between two dilapidated buildings. Funny how I hadn't noticed this place before despite the fact I travel along this way toward the South Side nearly every day. It was an odd looking establishment called The Dhamira Curio and Gift Shop. I say it was odd, not because it had a strange shape or color, but simply because it didn't seem to belong where it was. The South Loop was in the middle of a renaissance, and these few buildings were all that remained of its inglorious past. This kind of store didn't seem right for the area for some reason. It was almost as if someone had plucked the small building from the North Side, found a space that fit and dropped it right where it was now. Quite honestly I didn't care; as long as it had everything needed for the party and could deliver.

That, plus my raging desire to hold Juliana in my arms again, was all that concerned me at the moment.

"Let's try this place," I said, pulling the car over.

Upon entering the store I felt as if we had entered a time warp, for it clearly was divided into two sections. To the left there were all kinds of odd looking items for sale: dream catchers, ceramic kittens, ships in bottles, hand-knitted throw pillows, designer pottery and antique touchier lamps. On the other were gift cards, streamers, table cloths with matching napkins, paper plates, plastic silverware, candles and balloons. Lots of balloons. Though the shop was neat and tastefully decorated, it was like walking between past and present, with a single aisle that separated the two.

The bell jingled a second time as the door closed and clearly announced our arrival, yet there was no one behind the counter. Julie walked along the dividing line of the store, scanning items from both sides of the aisle. The further back she went, the more she reminded me of Jonah from Moby Dick, for it seemed as if she were being swallowed up in the belly of this strange store. It had an alluring, yet definitive quality about it that made me wonder why I chose this store in the first place. These were items you could find almost anywhere, yet there seemed to be a mystery behind them that made me quite nervous. I couldn't put my finger on it, but all I knew was I wanted to get this over with and get out of here.

"Can I help you?" asked a voice from behind me.

I turned and was face to face with an elderly black man, roughly five foot ten, with an unkempt salt and pepper beard and pock marks across his face. His eyes appeared tired, worn, and the longer I stared at him I could clearly see the right one was brown, the left gray. His glare reminded me of my grandmother, who gave me a similar look when she knew I had just lied to her.

"Good afternoon, sir. I'm Dr. Raymond Chandler," I said. "I'm here to buy some things for my daughter's birthday party in two weeks."

Juliana heard me talking and joined us, giving the frail looking man an innocent nod. He eyed us both, a thin smile coating his leathery face. Now I really wanted out of this place.

"I see. And how old is your daughter, Dr. Chandler?" The Merchant asked.

"She's turning ten. It seems like yesterday I was holding her in my arms and already she's thinking of high school. Where does the time go, eh?"

My feeble attempt at striking a conversation went nowhere. This guy hardly seemed alive; he stood perfectly still, closed his eyes and took a series of deep breaths. I don't quite know how to explain it, but it felt as if he were actually trying to smell us. He did it with such effort that I wondered if he was actually successful, when suddenly he opened his eyes and smiled. His entire demeanor changed just like that.

"Now then, approximately how many people do you expect at her party?"

"Oh, I'd say roughly thirty-five to forty-five people. We'd like to have the usual – matching plates, napkins, streamers. No hats. Many of her friends are going, so she thinks she's too old for that kind of thing. Oh, but she does want balloons though. I guess she wasn't quite willing to give up everything."

The Merchant showed us a variety of colors and patterns, which I was quite happy with. Desiree's favorite color was red, so everything I chose centered on that. The Merchant was quite good with his recommendations and I was more than satisfied once we settled on everything. He also told us he could handle the cake and ice cream, so we chose a red velvet cake layered and frosted with whipped butter cream frosting and homemade strawberry ice cream. I made the arrangements to have everything delivered three hours in advance of the party. Isabella had already asked Juliana if she would help set everything up while she took Desiree and Chelsea out until everything was ready.

Though the man was a bit strange, the experience worked out once everything got going. The price was reasonable and I gave him all of my personal information so he knew where to go. Until now he'd hardly said a word to Juliana. In fact, at times he seemed to posture himself as if she weren't there, and it wasn't until everything was done when he actually looked at her. I think she got the message that he wasn't interested in getting to know her, so she walked to the right of the store and glanced at his large selection of balloons. As I counted my money he took a moment to step away from the counter and join Juliana, as she came across his "Happy Face" collection.

"You like these balloons, do you miss?" he asked.

"Yes, I do. My parents bought these for me when I was just a little girl. I don't know – there's something about them that always put me in a good mood."

"Yes indeed, miss – I agree. This Happy Face that you see before you is a universal symbol of joy, good tidings like that of religious figures with 'half-smiles' of joy and peace. Some scholars would say that the Happy Face depicts a part of the human collective unconscious. In reality, it's but one portion of a vast range of emotions that human beings choose to show the world. During celebratory occasions, its primary role is for happiness, but I think there is far more that these balloons could show, given a different set of circumstances."

I stopped counting my money, immediately thinking this man was clearly out of his mind.

"So are you telling us that balloons can reflect our inner selves?" I asked him.

He gave me that "stare" once again, nodding in agreement.

"Just as a mirror can accurately reflect our outside appearance, I believe the face on these balloons can reflect what we're thinking and feeling deep inside our souls."

"Almost like a physical representation of our individual conscience, right?"

The strange old man nodded again. "Exactly!"

Juliana turned away from him; she twisted her face as tightly as she could to keep from laughing at the nutty Merchant. My teeth clamped down hard on my tongue, but evidently I was too late. He saw me on the verge of laughter and clearly wasn't amused.

"That'll be one-fifty, please!" he said, handing me my receipt.

His movements from that point on were crisp and tight, no longer the relaxed salesman that had given us great ideas for Desiree's party. I felt bad in hurting his feelings, but what an absurd thing to say! Who on earth would believe that balloons could have a conscience of their own? At the time I just blew it off, but now I'm starting to realize what a mistake it was to laugh at that old Merchant. If I were to ever see him again, I would tell him I'm sorry.

He rang up the sale and assured me that everything would be delivered to my home by the requested time, so Juliana and I made our way toward the front door. Before walking outside, I took one last glance at The Merchant, who stood by the Happy Face balloons, his body fixed in an odd looking pose.

He appeared as if he were listening to something being whispered into his ear.

***

May 19 – 12:17pm

The delivery for Desiree's party had arrived just after twelve, and once again, Isabella had taken my daughter and Chelsea to the movies and out shopping for the day, so I had plenty of time to get things ready. My dining area resembled something out of Romper Room, but still I thought it would work for my now teenage daughter. The cake and ice cream were in the refrigerator, along with several trays of chicken fingers, buffalo wings, jalapeno poppers and mozzarella sticks, which were to be heated up starting a half hour prior to the arrival of our guests. We had plenty of pop, lemonade and fruit punch to last us a lifetime, and I made sure our video camera was fully charged so the entire event could be recorded. For months, Desiree had told her mother and me how much she was looking forward to her birthday. Perhaps I had forgotten what it was like to be her age, but to her I supposed it meant that she was close to entering the one stage all fathers around the world hate more than anything – womanhood. My own dad told me many years ago what it was like when he had my sister and how difficult it was seeing daddy's little girl turn to some average guy. My dad would often compare the men she brought home to himself, wondering if he were a good enough role model for her so that she would find the proper man to marry. Fathers never believe their daughters are marrying the right man for that very reason, and because of it they are always suspicious. He told me a long time ago that I would understand someday if I ever had a daughter of my own. Perhaps now I was learning the truth for the first time.

Everything was ready to go. There was a section for gifts and the closets were all cleaned out to hang up jackets. I also sorted through her music lists on her laptop computer so I knew which crappy songs to play for her friends. Quite honestly I despise the talentless artists of today who insist on producing loud, obnoxious music. I'm from the old school, so I grew up listening to real talent, like the O'Jays, Earth Wind & Fire, The Commodores, Roy Ayers, The Ohio Players, Gladys Knight and the Pips. These people could all sing and write their own lyrics, not "cheat" the system by using beat machines and samples like Lil' Wayne, Swizz Beats and Timbaland. By far, the person I couldn't stand more than anyone was this new artist, KeKe. Awful in my opinion, and while she had a lot of songs I loved to hate, the one that took the cake was "Prima Donna." Desiree would dance around, "poppin' it like it's hot" as she liked to say, imitating KeKe and the rest of her half-dressed dancers in that ridiculous video. The folks from my day were trained musicians who were trendsetters for generations to come, not these lousy, fly-by-night chipmunks of today. Despite it all, however, I decided to deal with it for Desiree, and just for the occasion I actually bought ear plugs in case the bass got out of control. Demanding that she turn off her music on her special day was not an option for me, being the loving dad I had always been to her. Oh the joys of parenthood!

Now that there was nothing else left to do, I put in a call to Juliana, who slipped out the back of her house and made her way over to me, where we made love on my couch in the basement for the better part of an hour. While it was obvious that she and I had always clicked, there was something about this day, this moment, which separated it from the rest. With Juliana in my arms I felt as if I were flying high above the clouds with her, becoming one and the same in every way possible. That afternoon had been a nice experience for both of us.

"Fantastic," she said, nuzzling up close to me while I tried to catch my breath.

I laughed and kissed her forehead. Both of us remained silent for several minutes. I could hear our hearts beat.

"What are we gonna do, babe? The two of us are so in need. Can it go anyplace besides this?"

Juliana didn't answer. Shortly thereafter she began crying.

"Every night I lay next to Elijah, staring at him while he sleeps and wondering why I continue living the way I do. He's so cruel to me and hits me in front my daughter. Sometimes I think Chelsea is embarrassed to have me as a mother and would rather spend time with Isabella to avoid being near me. What makes it even worse...is I actually like Isabella. I consider her a friend..."

She pauses, looks directly at me. "...meanwhile I'm fucking her husband every chance I can get! What kind of friend is that?"

Tears continued streaming down her cheeks. I tried my best to comfort her, but I didn't know what to do or say that could make things better. Here were the both of us, stealing moments like these to be with one another, completely unhappy in our marriages despite having everything a person could possibly want – a nice home, cars, careers, money. But as I've found over the years, especially having been married to Isabella for so long, was that none of these material things could make up for what the human heart had needed most. I loved Isabella, but was never in-love with her. I loved her enough to get married, to have our beautiful daughter and to give them as much as I could in terms of financial security and stability, but what I could not provide for her was my heart. I was aware of her dislike of sex from the very beginning; I also knew I needed someone that was emotionally on the same wavelength as me – and early on it was clear that she was much more guarded than I could handle. And despite being aware of all this, I still married her anyway, being arrogant enough to think I could change her into the person that I wanted. Now, several years later, I'm stuck in a rut of my own doing. All of this was my fault, and now Juliana was a major part of my mess.

"Simple, right? We just leave our spouses and live happily ever after," I remarked aloud.

Juliana chuckled. "Yeah...simple!"

For some reason, despite all the confusion and uncertainty in both our lives, I felt it necessary to get something off my chest. It couldn't wait any longer.

"I love you, Julie," I said.

Not missing a beat, she said: "I love you too, Ray."

Now what?

***

3:36pm

With Juliana gone and me having to clean up, I did a quick batch of laundry, i.e. the sheets and towels we had used earlier. Now it was time to put on a different face and slip into the usual Dr. Raymond Chandler act – that of a proud husband and father. I had become good at moving between the two roles over the years, though I hated it beyond belief. In many ways I felt like an actor who was playing a role completely unlike me in real life. I remember once reading an article about Forrest Whitaker after he portrayed Idi Amin in The Last King of Scotland. The article said that when he was finally done with the role, he took a shower and screamed as the water rushed over his body. He said he screamed and screamed because he needed to get Amin "out of his system," having played such a vile role. That's exactly how I feel sometimes. I so wanted to get rid of this dual life of mine; it was making me so unhappy at times that I couldn't focus on what was in front of me. Some might think I was in a mid-life crisis, wondering what I had made of my life thus far and whether I had accomplished anything of substance. I would probably say they were right – I was struggling for truth, for change. For something. Anything. I just didn't know what at this point. The only thing I was certain of was that I couldn't continue much longer the way I was going.

The laundry was done and I had roughly an hour and a half or so before guests would begin to arrive, so I was about to take a shower when I saw something inside one of the paper bags from the gift shop. It was a small envelope that had my name on it, and from the feel of it there was something round on the inside. I ripped open the package and a small necklace with a silver chain slid into my palm. I turned the circular pendant over with my index finger and saw a yellow "Happy Face" staring back at me, just like the ones I saw at The Merchant's shop a few weeks ago. Inside the torn envelope was a small folded piece of paper that simply said "Wear Me." Naturally I figured The Merchant had done this on purpose, given all that nonsense about Happy Faces with consciences, so I took the chain, threw it in the garbage and took the trash bag out to the alley for today's four o'clock pickup.

If I knew then what I know now, I would never have thrown that necklace away!

***

3:51pm

I was just beginning to get dressed, so I decided to keep it casual and wear a short sleeve shirt due to the unseasonably warm weather outside. Fortunately I had just serviced my central air conditioning, so if having the windows open became too much for our guests, I could close them and turn the system on. Already the humidity was beginning to feel as if it were June instead of May. Isabella and I preferred having a cool house, so I always made sure I stayed on top of the service work for our central air. Believe it or not, it was one of the few things both of us actually agreed on.

I had just finished brushing my teeth and slipped on my gym shoes when suddenly I heard a loud racket coming from outside my bedroom window. Thinking it was some obnoxious kid, I rushed to the window and screamed "knock it off" when I saw there were no kids outside at all. In fact, there were no cars out front whatsoever. The only thing that was there was a single red balloon that hovered directly over my front lawn exactly at eye level. There was something written on the front of it that I couldn't quite see from this distance, but one thing I could tell for sure was the red balloon appeared to pulsate from the heavy bass of the music. I was motionless, stunned. I couldn't believe what I was looking at, and almost as if the balloon had read my mind, it began to float very slowly toward me, the heavy "thump, thump" of the music became clearer, more audible.

Of all things - it was the music to "Prima Donna" by KeKe.

The balloon continued to pulsate, that awful sound became louder and louder as I covered my ears; the beat rattled my brain causing me to lose my balance. I had to lean against the window to keep from falling over as I searched the room for the ear plugs I had recently bought for Desiree's party, but my vision had become blurry because the entire house seemed to shake around me. I dropped down to one knee, but eventually recovered well enough to close the window. Though the sound was muffled my drapes were swaying to the beat as if someone were blowing against them. I had no idea what this was all about, but one thing was certain – I must not open that window again. The balloon continued to hover about, the beat pounded away outside and I could see it gradually turning in front of the window until I saw the makings of a face. It appeared to be exactly like the Happy Face from The Merchant's store, except it wasn't happy at all. In fact, the balloon had an ugly scowl on it and appeared to bare fangs at me!

"What the fuck?" I shouted, as the face began to rub itself against my window, pushing against the panes as if it were trying to get inside.

The balloon backed away from the window and I could see it floating down the south end of my house until it found another one that was open. The sound was louder than before; the balloon continued to grow in size, vibrating to the sound as KeKe's shrill voice kept screeching on and on: *"I'm a Prima Donna, baby, gimme, gimme some! I'm a Prima Donna boy, better gimme some!"*

After I slammed my guest-room window shut, the balloon once again tried to push its way in, only to float away in search of another open window. I found myself running around the entire top level of the house, slamming all my windows and locking them – much to the chagrin of the balloon, which had now grown as large as a beach ball. Angry scowl intact, still pulsating and quite determined, it suddenly descended, making its way down to the first floor. I took off, running so fast that I nearly tripped down my staircase, and as I made it to my foyer the bass blared in my ears once again, so I shut every window, starting from the front room all the way to the back of the house. The last one I had closed was over my kitchen sink.

The balloon was huge; the mouth on its face was as nasty looking as ever, though for once it appeared as if it had given up. It didn't take its eyes off of me as we stared at one another for what felt like several minutes until it turned away from the window and looked around, studying the perimeter of my backyard as if it were trying to formulate a plan.

What the hell was it doing now? Finally it turned back to me and bared its fangs; the scowl turned into a wicked smile.

And then it flew away, the sound of the bass gradually faded out.

I uncovered my ears, an unfounded sense of accomplishment swept over me like a gentle breeze. I checked all the windows in the kitchen but saw no trace of my nefarious, 'helium-filled' nemesis. My short sleeve oxford shirt was soaked from front to back, as well as under my armpits; I was wheezing as if I were in between rounds of a heavyweight fight. Sweat continued to drip down my forehead as I poured a cold glass of water, rubbing the drink across my face and taking a healthy swig until I heard the ice clink on the bottom. The level of exhaustion I felt for such a short occurrence was incredible. This whole thing couldn't have been more than four or five minutes tops, but what I saw was so weird, so unbelievable that it had literally worn me out beyond belief. Of all things, I had just been threatened by a fucking BALLOON? A red balloon with an evil look had menaced me in my own house? I clearly must be going mad! My mind was still trying to wrap around that idea as I thought of the conversation Juliana and I had with The Merchant a few weeks prior:

"Just as a mirror can accurately reflect our outside appearance, I believe the face on these balloons can reflect what we're thinking and feeling deep inside our souls."

That nutty old guy tried to tell us that Happy Face balloons showed only one of several kinds of emotions, as if it were actually a conscience! What a totally preposterous idea on his part, however – how could I explain what I had just seen with my own eyes? Either I must be a textbook candidate for an insane asylum or I actually had seen a balloon attempt to attack me. I was desperate, walking along the brink of sanity when I remembered the necklace I had found just about an hour ago. The note gave me specific instructions to wear it, and not only did I ignore what I was told to do, I threw the thing away. I checked my watch and it was just after four.

I quickly ran to my backyard, keeping a close eye on the whereabouts of the red balloon, which was nowhere in sight. I checked the can in the alley and, of course, the trash had already been picked up. In fact, just as I headed back to my yard I saw the garbage truck going around the corner.

***

4:15pm

Still there was no sign of the red balloon, so I took a seat at my kitchen table. It was unusually warm inside the house, more than likely because all of my windows were now closed, so I went to turn on the central air-conditioning, but to no avail. The generator should have switched on, especially since I had the damn thing fixed just over a week ago, so I took another walk outside when I noticed a long, thin white string that dangled from the top of the generator. As I got closer to it, I could see remnants of something that had become jammed inside. There were several shredded parts of that oversized balloon stuck throughout the fan blades, plus there was the foul smell of burnt rubber that flared my nostrils causing me to sneeze. The string that was attached to the balloon had wrapped around the blades as well, making a trail down the side of the generator and across the sidewalk.

"Unbelievable," I remarked aloud. That damn balloon had intentionally stuck itself inside my central air conditioner and got all chewed up so I couldn't use it! And now that I was expecting guests I would HAVE to open all my windows in order to keep the place cool. The last thing I wanted was to have a house full of people with the windows shut.

What the hell was going on here? Am I going crazy? How was it possible for an inanimate object such as this to plot against me? I continued looking back and forth from the shredded mess to the end of the string, stunned. Then, almost as if could read my mind, that horrible pulsating rhythm filled my ears again, only this time the sound progressively became louder, deeper. The bass shook inside my head so much that my teeth felt on the verge of shattering; the noise hitting me as if I were in a heavyweight fight. I stumbled back to the kitchen, my vision blurry from the heavy pounding, and managed to shut the patio door, though it didn't kill the sound. The air was thick with that odious scent of rubber, and as I turned I could feel repeated blasts of hot air press hard against my face. A red balloon with a wide scowl had been waiting for me in my kitchen, and now that it had my attention it came after me, following me from room to room!

"I'm a Prima Donna, baby, gimme, gimme some! I'm a Prima Donna boy, better gimme some!"

I scrambled upstairs and shut myself inside the master bedroom, searching for my pellet gun. One year prior I had an infestation of squirrels inside my attic, and one day when I tried to get rid of the nest I was nearly bitten, so the pellet gun came in handy in scaring them away long enough to have the hole patched up. Fortunately I kept the gun close by, and today it would serve a new purpose. It was still loaded, so I opened the door to our bathroom and lay in wait, knowing eventually it would come around looking for me. This time I would have it cornered!

As I sat on the floor I could feel the deep bass push hard against my back, gradually becoming convinced it knew I was there. For quite a while it held its position, then moved along the hallway and entered the bathroom. The pungent odor of the balloon pushed its way around the corner until the thing itself had finally become visible. I was scared shitless, but held firm just long enough until I was certain the balloon wasn't going anywhere. The pellet gun behind my back, I shook uncontrollably while the balloon seemed pleased by my fear as it began to stretch itself in front of me. Its mouth grew wide, the frown became more pronounced. Sinister. Evil.

It was now or never!

I drew the gun and fired. A loud bang that sounded like the tire of a semi-truck exploding on a highway had caused my ears to ring. An acrid smell, worse than the one from earlier, filled the room and pieces of rubber were everywhere, and just before I could open the windows I heard the generator to my central air conditioning turn on. Though I had quite a mess to clean up, there was just enough time to take another shower and set up Desiree's party. But in the end, I was indeed grateful that it was all over.

I had won the battle against the red balloon. Or so I thought.

***

5:57 pm

The party was now in full swing. Desiree had arrived at 5:30 with my wife and Chelsea to what she thought was an empty house, but little did she know it was packed to the gills with neighborhood friends, parents and relatives. Roughly forty people came, all lying in wait for her arrival. I truly was amazed at the turnout. My daughter was quite a popular, yet unassuming young girl who was mature beyond her years and there's no doubt in my mind that she would go on to do great things. She's driven, but balances that high determination with a sense of fair play, which let me know whatever was in her sights she would earn honestly. I'm relieved to know that I have a child who will achieve her goals. It makes everything so much easier on us as parents.

I also couldn't help but admire how Isabella handles Desiree. Many of my female patients who are mothers often complain about their daughters as if they are in competition with them. I know that sounds ridiculous, but it's true! Not long ago I was counseling a mother in her early forties who was having an all-out war with her twelve-year-old over who would actually get to sit in her husband's lap at night. I nearly fell out of my chair when she said her daughter called her a bitch, took her daddy's beer and splashed it in her mother's face. I guess I shouldn't find any of that funny, but in comparison to my wife and daughter, it all seemed like night and day.

Just looking at the two of them interacting brings such joy to my heart, followed by a deepening sense of guilt because of my deceptive behavior. My wife and my mistress stood no more than five feet from one another but were millions of miles apart in terms of my personal affections. I cared for my wife, but I was in love with Juliana – not simply because I was sleeping with her, but because I knew deep in my heart that every aspect of my being had wanted her. I could imagine the two of us spending our lives together, building a house filled with love in all respects, taking long, relaxing vacations together. The two of us "vibe" like trumpet players in a jazz band, speaking volumes without ever opening our mouths. That's the kind of closeness I've always desired but never have been able to find. I didn't know what I could do, but somehow I needed to figure out a way to be with her. That strange story she shared with me about "being Isabella's friend" didn't sound right to me at all. I'm afraid if I don't do something soon, make some kind of drastic move before it was too late, I might lose her. And as I pondered the possibilities for the umpteenth time, I arrived exactly back where I was at the beginning.

Stuck. Unsure. Horny. Trapped. And miserable.

Isabella tapped me on the shoulder. I was in such a daze from all the activity in the house that I hadn't noticed she had been standing next to me. Who knows how long she had been there.

"Ray, yoo-hoo!" she yodeled, finally getting my attention. I felt like I had just awakened.

"Oh, sorry hon. I'm a bit tired is all. Getting everything together for this party took more out of me than I thought it would." She kissed me on the cheek. This is what all these years being married now meant – a tight nudge on the cheek that hardly left a trace of moisture, let alone lipstick. Woody Woodpecker could give me a harder peck than that!

"You and Juliana really did a fantastic job with all of the decorations, honey. I'm glad I asked her to go with you."

"Me too," I nodded, thinking of our tryst from earlier. As my father used to say, "I can be a real 'sum-bitch' when I wanna be!"

"But there's one thing that you forgot to order, sweetie."
SWEETIE?

"What's that?"

She waved around the dining room. Kids, parents and something in between were everywhere chatting up a storm.

"You forgot to order balloons, silly!"

That's when I looked finally noticed it. Indeed she was right! There were no balloons in the room at all.

"But that doesn't make sense, Izzie. We ordered balloons as part of the package. I guess he forgot to bring them."

"Well if I were you, sweetie (there's that sweetie thing again), I would call him and complain, especially if you paid for it."

I agreed and just as I was about to make a phone call I could barely hear my doorbell ring above all the chatter and loud music. I answered it and to my surprise, standing in front of me was The Merchant.

"Wow! I was just about to call you, sir," I remarked. An odd looking smirk covered his wrinkled, leathery face.

"You were calling about the balloons, right? My apologies, Dr. Chandler. It wasn't until I completed my deliveries for the day that I realized I had forgotten to deliver them and...uh..."

The old man looked at me as if he were searching for something. He asked: "Dr. Chandler, did you find that necklace I brought you?"

I swallowed hard, nodded. "Yes, but I threw it away."

A strange smile crept across The Merchant's face. "Has anything...strange...happened to you today?"

Suddenly I felt sick to my stomach: "Yes."

His amused glance told me all I needed to know. There were guests walking all around us in my front room, so he grabbed my arm, pulled me close and whispered in my ear: "Leave this house, Dr. Chandler. You didn't believe, and now you are in grave danger."

I nodded, and held my breath as The Merchant stepped onto the front porch and reached for something just off to the left of my door. He looked at whatever he had and re-entered my house, handing me what appeared to be three dozen "smiley-face" balloons in various colors.

"Drop these off to your wife and go."

I stared at the balloons, too afraid to move a muscle. The Merchant slapped my arm, trying to get my attention. "DR. CHANDLER, DID YOU HEAR ME?!"

"Yes, yes – I heard you." He gave me his best "you just fucked up" look and left me to fend for myself. My daughter and Chelsea saw what I had before I could dump them off to Isabella.

"Wow, Daddy! Look at all those balloons!" she exclaimed. Even now, Desiree loved balloons. At age eight she started to turn her nose up at them, but during a trip to the Wisconsin Dells we took a hot air balloon ride together. She's loved them ever since.

Desiree reached for one, but I held back. "Uh uh! Not until we open presents later!"

"Awwwww! Can't I have one now, Daddy? Pleeeeeeeeease? It's my birthday!"

Now what father could possibly say no to that? Especially a sucker-dad like me?

"Okay, one for you and one for Chels..."

As I was about to hand Desiree a red balloon the "smiley" side of it faced me. Suddenly the face stretched from a smile into a frown. Teeth started appearing on the balloon as it glared at me with a frightful look. I took a fast glance at the others in the bunch and they too had begun to scowl at me in a way that was even angrier than the one from earlier today. I tried to hand the entire bunch of them to my daughter so I could make my escape, but together they blocked me from her and Chelsea, forcing me into a corner. The strings that held all of them together wrapped itself tightly around my hand, making it impossible for me to let them go. And once they had me firmly secured against the wall, that horrible music pounded my ears once again:

"I'm a Prima Donna, baby, gimme, gimme some! I'm a Prima Donna boy, better gimme some!"

The sound was bad enough with one of them, but with three dozen balloons it was so loud that I lost my balance. Up seemed down to me. The entire room began spinning. I puked. From the corner of my eye I could see my daughter becoming upset. Several of our guests, as well as my wife Isabella came running, probably thinking I was having a seizure or something. I tried to crawl past the balloons, but they actually blocked me from her and converged on top of me, pulsating and growling like rabid dogs. A few of them nipped at my ankles and arms – wherever there was open flesh they started to feast on me as if I were the catch of the day.

Indeed I was.

I screamed and thrashed about, but they refused to let me go – that goddamn song booming in my ears until I could barely hear anything else. I felt seconds away from bursting an eardrum when the music quieted and my own voice started yelling at me: "TELL HER! TELL HER! TELL HER! TELL HER! TELL HER!"

I couldn't take it any longer. Everyone stared at me as if I were out of my mind, rolling around with balloons in my hand while only I knew what was happening. The noise and screaming by the balloons had to stop, so I simply did exactly what they told me to do: "ISABELLA, I AM HAVING AN AFFAIR WITH JULIANA!"

The music stopped at once, and one by one the balloons exploded – the sound reminiscent of popcorn popping in a microwave. People ducked for cover, screaming, grabbing their kids as bits of rubber and string blew everywhere until the very last one was gone. I finally stood up, covered in the carnage. My daughter and Chelsea were in tears. My wife was fuming.

"Get out of this house right now, Raymond!"

Without question, I simply turned and did as I was told.

***

Eight Years Later

That night I drove around for about an hour and decided to head over to my office, where I usually kept one change of clothes and a few toiletry items. I was smart enough to have a shower built into the bathroom and there was a comfortable leather couch for me to sleep on, though I'm sure you know that sleep was the last thing I did.

I had really screwed up. My daughter was a basket case for months and Isabella immediately filed for divorce. It's bad enough to get caught having an affair, but for it to all come out like it did? I was certain, the humiliation factor notwithstanding, that my marriage was beyond saving. But to be honest, I actually didn't care that she and I called it quits, for it went on far longer than it really should have, and my complacency is what ultimately caused this to happen. Once I came to that realization, I thought again of what The Merchant had said when Juliana and I were in his store: *"Just as a mirror can accurately reflect our outside appearance, I believe the face on these balloons can reflect what we're thinking and feeling deep inside our souls."*

I remember the two of us laughing at the idea, but after what happened, I found it to be almost prophetic. We had doubted The Merchant, but he couldn't have been more correct. Those balloons were an inverse of my angry self – upset that my spirit had settled for mediocrity for so long. I don't mean that Isabella was a mediocre person; she was a wonderful woman in her own way. But the truth was we were never good for each other, and I'm sure – despite all that took place – she was somewhat relieved that the time to move on had finally presented itself. In my own strange way, I was grateful to the balloons for what they had done. I even went so far as to attempt to thank The Merchant for what happened, but when I went to look for his store all I found was an empty lot filled with broken glass, dirt and crumbled bricks that had been sealed off by the city. It was as if the store had never been there.

Had I? Had Juliana?

For such a long time I moved about like the living dead, a corpse that mindlessly trudged along doing the same things I had done for years: going to work, going home, paying bills, putting on a front for everyone around me. I suppose all of us end up in that kind of rut where our lives are reduced to a select few things that we do on a weekly basis, but what I had been doing for almost the entirety of my marriage with Isabella was indeed a shame. Like in George Romero's "Night of the Living Dead," I was the man wandering through the cemetery, arms out, eyes rolled to the back of my head, searching for places familiar to me in a state of utter boredom. Back then my life was contrived, artificial. And after losing my house, half of our assets and nearly my dignity, I had paid the heavy price for my mistakes. But finally I woke up!

It took a lot of therapy, but eventually my daughter began to show love for me again. We took it slow and gradually came back together over time, just in time for her high school graduation. That summer she was accepted to The University of Illinois at Urbana-Champaign and decided pre-med was her choice of major. She let it slip that she wanted to specialize in child and adolescent psychiatry;

given the valuable counseling she experienced first-hand. I was quite proud of her.

Isabella remarried and appeared to be happy again – an inner glow so visible and so natural that she actually came to forgive me, and even acknowledged that she understood why I had cheated on her. That certainly helped me to recover my own self-worth after that horrible ordeal. At least I was no longer the 'total' scumbag that I was made out to be. You take your victories as you get them, I guess.

As for Juliana, she decided to stay with Elijah, who continued to abuse her after all that happened between us. Then one day I received a phone call from Desiree that Elijah had passed away. Heart attack.

Couldn't have happened to a nicer person!

I haven't seen nor spoken to Juliana since that night. Many times I've wanted to call her, but figured it was best to stay away, at least that's what I had long believed, until one day who should stop by my office but Chelsea. Now eighteen years old, she shared with me how relieved she was that Elijah was finally out of their lives for good. Juliana once believed her daughter was embarrassed of her, but that couldn't be further from the truth. Chelsea felt helpless in protecting her mother from "that monster," as she referred to her dad and told me she was jealous of Desiree for having such a kind father.

"I was never upset with you once I found out," she told me. "The only time I saw her smile was when you were someplace nearby. I still remember that to this day."

***

Juliana lived in the same house after all of these years. When Chelsea last visited she urged me to call, saying her mother would love to hear from me. For the past week the temptation to call her had intensified, but I came up with every excuse in the book as to why I shouldn't do it, until one day I was at the Evergreen Plaza Mall on the far south side doing some shopping for Desiree's nineteenth birthday. I happened to walk past "Let's Party - Gifts and Novelties" on the lower level and decided to take a walk inside, wandering aimlessly through the aisles until I came to the balloon section. An entire wall of "smiley-face" balloons of all colors stared blankly back at me, grins firmly in place, expressions pleasant as could be. A woman happened to walk by with her son just as I had acquiesced to my adopted latex confidants, saying aloud: "okay, okay...I promise to do the right thing as soon as possible!" I saw the lady grab her kid and rush toward the front of the store, looking back at me as if to say "this guy must be nuts!" Perhaps she was right.

I immediately walked out of the store, found the nearest Starbuck's and took a seat. In one hand was Juliana's number, in the other was my cell phone. "You know what you must do," I could hear those damned balloons tell me over and over again, but this time around I decided not to doubt their infinite wisdom, even though technically they were voiceless and brainless. I also came to accept that it was me, not the balloons, doing the talking. I no longer needed them because now I am the master of my own fate. It's time to step up to the plate and take control.

So without further delay - I took a deep breath, dialed the number and waited patiently for my soul mate to answer. As I did, some new song by KeKe piped through the speakers - something about *"do me 'gin baby like ya' did me last night,"* or something like that.

To be honest, I actually liked it.

CLOWNS

The Show

This place is crazy packed, Yo! I'm on stage doing my thing, just like I always do. With the Mike in my hand, I'm prowling the stage like a soldier with Sam Lucas, aka DJ Sabotage, cuttin' up the beats right on time. He and I have been in the rap game for years, ever since we were shorties coming up in the Gardens. We had that telepathy thing going, him and me, so it was rare we ever spoke to each other while performing. A quick glance was all it took. If I needed a breath, he'd take over and hit the crowd with some tricks until I was ready. Half our show was impromptu shit, never the same thing twice. We'd do the usual thing the crowd came to see, and just like that, we'd hit 'em up with something they ain't never seen before. That was customary with us – always turning the rap game on its ear, making waves rather than riding them. Niggas would check out our shit tonight and copy our style by tomorrow. That's just how it was, Yo! When you're running things as long as me and Sabo have, everyone wants to be down – even if they were straight hatin' you. It didn't matter. Fools wanna eat, so they suck that shit up and do what they gotta do. Period.

At first I thought the show was gonna be weak as hell. I really did, Yo! Even Sabo wasn't sure what to do when I first hit the stage. It was our thing to not see each other until show time. Call it superstition or whatever, but we viewed it as bad luck, just like the bride not wanting to see the groom before a wedding, right? Whoa, hold on! Ain't no homo shit going on with us or nothing like that, just business. We operate better when we're more relaxed so we could give the crowd a show. That's how you keep your fans happy, by putting out quality product. Any third-rate dope dealer on the street would tell you that. And if niggas keep putting out good product, niggas keep gettin' paid. Besides, I got responsibilities I gotta take care of, you know? I just bought my moms a new crib out in Tinley Park and put her on my payroll, so she's handling my personal affairs for me. My sister's in her second year at Loyola University. She wants to be a doctor someday, and that shit ain't cheap, you know what I'm saying? Plus, I got me a Shorty of my own that I'm taking care of right now - William, Jr., or 'Lil Man as my sister likes to call him. He's gonna be a heartbreaker like his bad ass daddy someday, so I've got him to think about too. Not to mention all the other stuff I keep funded by spitting rhymes on stages like this all over the world. So I have to do all this, know what I mean? So much depends on it, and I'm gonna do whatever it takes to keep things fresh. But like I said earlier, even though me and Sabo like to add a new dimension to our show, this thing I'm doing today actually took the cake:

"I'm clownin' motherfucker, I'm clownin' motherfucker, and fa 'sho ain't messin' around, motherfucker!"

It's all about delivery, see? If you get on stage and say some shit with feeling, people will buy into it. And just like I told you - me and Sabo don't need to talk to each other, we know exactly the job that must be done. When they first saw me hit the stage, no one said a word. In fact, some of them niggas was laughing at how I looked. But then Sabo started banging those hot tracks and the next thing you know I ripped 'em good. It's been a full hour and the crowd is still going crazy. We haven't done any of our other songs since I got started. Freestyle baby, that's all it's been thus far. And if I know Sabo like I do, I'm sure he's recording everything I'm saying right now so we can hook it up later back in the studio. Our manager is gonna work up a whole new marketing campaign for our next CD. And it's gonna work, no doubt!

"This ain't bullshit, homey! No silly tricks, no zaps, no flips, just GATs here, homey!"

I don't know why this happened to me; maybe it's my true calling. Something as harmless as 'Lil Man's toy has totally changed my life around. I look so different, my Moms wouldn't recognize me. In fact, she's looking at me right now, totally horrified at my hair and face. She saw me come on stage, tripping over my own big ass feet, thinking I was playing the part. Truth is, I wasn't playing at all. My feet swole up so big that after every fourth of fifth step I'd damn near break my neck, making this funny 'squeak' sound wherever I moved. Know what, though? I don't give a fuck, and hope I don't change back any time soon. I'll stay like this as long as I'm making this new look work for me. Why should I go back to wearing hoodies and bling and make my pants sag damn near to the ground when I'm blazin' a new trail with what I got on? I'm gonna get paid, player! And like I told you, me and Sabo are innovators. We set the trend, everybody else follows.

Know what I'm saying?

***

Three Hours Before the Show

William Robinson, known on stage as "Big Will", sat alone in his dressing room scribbling in his notebook, a practice that he had become legendary for over the years. No matter where Big Will went, he always carried four things: a black wallet, a blackberry, a black Paper Mate pen and a black Mead notepad, one that was usually small enough to slide in his back pocket. This was a practice taught to him by his mother, Anna Mae Robinson, a former schoolteacher who currently handled Will's personal affairs.

"I'm comin' at cha, hittin' hard and fas, like my nigga Mike Jordan, dunkin' on ya ass! Yeah, I like that shit," he whispered to himself, nodding in approval. He continued writing.

When Will was young, his mother would read books to him on a vast array of subjects: black history, detective stories, poetry. By the time Will was five, he had memorized several poems by Harlem Renaissance legends Langston Hughes, Claude McKay and Countee Cullen, and at family gatherings he would stand before everyone and recite a new poem that he had learned with a power and sense of confidence rarely seen by someone so young. Sensing that she had a prodigy in her midst, Moms encouraged her nine year old son to write his own poetry and bought his very first Mead notepad and Paper Mate pen. Both Black. She did that intentionally, a symbolic gesture that implied the inherent responsibility that these powerful words, written by a talented black child, should be kept 'black' as a reminder of who he was and where he had come from.

Will was in performance mode. Inside his head he could hear Sabo playing music, so he started 'spitting' lyrics in front of a mirror, imagining he was at an old school battle and the person in front of him was the enemy. Earlier he told us about the importance of delivery, that if you spoke with authority you could demand the listener's respect. That was an art that he practiced repeatedly, so even if he forgot a line it would hardly be noticeable. Will's idol was LL Cool J because of his versatility in his approach to rhyming. LL could bring the pain or be the smoothest player on the planet, depending on his lyrics. I'm Bad was an example of LL's hard persona, while I Need Love showed more of the dashing, debonair side of his delivery. Will didn't bite his idol's stage presence, but understood how to read the crowd and project a certain image at will. It took practice, lots of it. He was giving it a go right now.

"Still trying to be a thug, are we?" said Moms, holding 'Lil Man in her arms as she entered the dressing room. She dropped a small shopping bag onto a plush black leather couch near the door.

Will stopped his 'performance' and smiled at her. "Hey momma, you know this keeps the bills paid. It's all an act."

"Yeah, well I wish you'd 'act' like somebody else. You know how I feel about all this."

Will frowned. "Mom, can we please not argue right now? I've gotta get ready for the show."

"Alright, alright...oh, I spoke to Gene. He's sending a limousine afterwards to take you to the Cotton Club for the after-party. Around eleven his driver will be waiting backstage, so you're all set. Your clothes for tonight are being pressed, so Felicia will drop them off to you."

Big Will rubbed his son's head: "What would I do without grandma, huh kiddo?"

Lil Man shrugged. So did his daddy, who was a walking collage of contradictions.

Despite the "gangsta" image that he had created for himself, Will had secretly funded minority scholarships in conjunction with the Chicago Public School System and the City Colleges of Chicago for underprivileged students. Youth centers across the city that once had been closed were re-opening, equipped with brand new computers, libraries and drug/gang-free playground facilities where the kids could learn and grow without fear of thugs from the neighborhood. Though he was never in a gang, Will knew a lot of gangbangers and managed to forge a pact with them not to come around the centers. In fact, some of his contacts were so high up in the ranks that they actually kept the areas clear. In exchange, Will gave away promotional copies of his mixtapes for the local crews. Small price to pay to enable the children's safety, and it proved to be worthwhile.

He also donated funds to the March of Dimes and the United Negro College Fund, plus co-sponsored events for Breast Cancer Awareness Month – his mother having been a recent cancer survivor. All of these things were ideas Will had come up with on his own, and though she was proud of all her son had accomplished with his life, she was upset that he felt the need to keep it all hidden from the public. He would tell her that he was a modest person who didn't want the personal accolades, but Moms knew better than that. Any mention of him appearing "soft" would tarnish his so-called image, and if he wouldn't be as popular as he now was. It was all a game. A game he had to play.

Moms hated every bit of it.

"Make sure you're ready to go when Felicia gets here, Will. We don't wanna have the riot we nearly had last night because you're too busy being 'fashionably late'. Understand?"

"Yes, ma'am. Can't believe it! I'm almost thirty and I'm still answering to my mother like I'm Lil Man's age."

The child shrugged his shoulders a second time. Moms smiled at both of them.

"Well maybe if you started listening to me I wouldn't have to repeat myself. Know what I'm sayin', homey?"

Will chuckled, shook his head. "Here we go again. Okay Ma, I know you don't like me cussin' and all that on stage, but look at us. We're rich now, no more living paycheck to paycheck. You won't ever have to work again. Angie can go to medical school. Lil Man here...he's gonna be all set by the time I get done with this thing. All of us ain't wantin' for..."

"AREN'T wanting," she interrupted. Will sighed.

"Mom, you know where I'm going with this. Why are you being this way?"

Moms approached her son, embraced him. "I'm sorry baby. I know I'm hard on you about this, but I can't help it. I feel the way I do for a reason."

Will nodded. "I know."

Moms sharply disagreed. "No you don't. If you understood you'd never do it in the first place."

She broke away from him, her head down. She faced the door, silent.

"I know that you are respected for what you do, and for that I'm very proud of you, Will."

He smiled. "Thanks, but what else?"

Moms turned, faced him. "The 'what else' is the cost of doing it. These kids look up to you, Will. They admire you, emulate everything you do. And you're leading them by example. I'm not saying you're telling them to tote guns and call each other the N-word, but because it's you they naturally try to act that way. They want to be you. That's where the problem lies."

"Momma, I'm no role model. I never claimed to be."

"Oh yes you are, Will. You may not think so, but you are. You're in the public eye. People buy your products. They say your words. They see your movies. You are very much a role model to them, son."

Will picked up his son and approached her. The look on his face reminded her of when he was Lil Man's age. Neither of them spoke for a while, until Moms said: "You're phenomenal to watch on stage, Will. Everyone's mesmerized by your presence, the power in which you speak. All that reading of poetry when you were a child, plus your own natural charisma, has made you as good as you are today. I just want you to use your gift responsibly instead of looking like a clown onstage. That's all."

Will was stunned. He never heard his mother use such words before to describe his act.

"Momma, you think I look like a clown? How could you say that to me?"

He put down Lil Man and walked away from her. Truly hurt.

"I'm sorry sweetie. I'm glad all this helps you do good things for people, but at what price? Your own self-respect? People died so you could live free of such vile words, like nigger. And if they think it's cool to say that word, then what was our struggle all about? I raised a talented young man, one who used to make his own identity stand out to others."

She approached her son, taking his hand. "And I know this same talented man can create a new image all his own."

Will nearly cried as she kissed his cheek. "I appreciate you taking care of us. You have a good heart; your momma's heart. But I'd rather work three jobs than make a fortune saying the things you do on stage."

Lil Man looked up at his father, their eyes locked. For the first time, Big Will wondered whether he was a good role model to his own son.

"Don't make any decisions now, Will. Just think about it, that's all."

And with that, she left both of her "men," staring at one another inside the lavish dressing room. Neither of them made a sound.

***

All around the Mulberry Bush
The monkey chased the weasel
The monkey stopped to pull up his sock
POP! goes the weasel

One Hour Later

A sound jarred him awake. Will nearly jumped out of bed, startled by Lil Man who was playing with his new toy – one that Moms bought for him earlier today. Will felt dizzy, his face and ears were burning as if he'd been inside a tanning booth. Nearly an hour ago he laid down for a nap, thinking the rest would do him some good, but now he woke up feeling as if he were sick. He wondered if some strange bug was going around. Now wasn't the time to be sick – not at the beginning of a twenty-three city tour!

He rubbed his eyes and yawned as Lil Man giggled and fiddled around with his new toy. While Will was asleep his son, supposedly taking a nap with his daddy, had gotten up and rummaged through the shopping bag that Moms left behind. The bag was thrown to the side, the words "The Dhamira Curio and Gift Shop" appeared in Old English text. Will examined the bag – there was no address or telephone number.

"Hey boy, whatcha doin' over there, huh?"

Lil Man faced his daddy, shrugged his shoulders and flashed his patented toothy smile.

Will felt lucky to have a son like Lil Man - an intelligent, gregarious child who seemed so at ease no matter what he was doing or who he was with. To this day Will couldn't understand why Kelli, his former wife, had decided to walk out on them. She claimed it was the lifestyle of being a celebrity wife that she couldn't handle, but to relinquish her parental rights was inexcusable in Will's mind. The truth was she never wanted to be a mother or wife. Her main goal was to have a man give her things and take her places, but Kelli had Will figured all wrong. She believed the hype, but what she found was a young man with an 'old soul' – someone who secretly wanted the big white house and two-car garage with the matching picket fence. Kelli wanted the sizzle of being in the spotlight: plenty of bling-bling, popped bottles of Cristal and luxury cruises to the Caribbean.

Her girlfriends told her to 'get paid' and keep her man happy, but playing the role of happy housewife wasn't in the cards for her. One day she packed her bags and walked out, Lil Man crying and begging for his mother. Who could resist such a pleasant young boy like this? One that everyone in Will's circle had adopted as their 'play cousin' and spoiled half to death? At first Will felt bad for his son. Later he realized it was best that she left. After all, you can't miss what was never there in the first place.

"What are you playing with, 'lil homey? Something Grandma bought for you?"

Lil Man nodded.

"Can I see your toy?"

Lil Man nodded again and turned around. Firmly clenched in his little hands was a vintage 1955 Jack-in-the-Box by Mattel Toy Company. The clown drooped lazily to one side; the clothing and face were worn but still quite visible. Like most of the Jack-in-the-Boxes from that era, this box wasn't made out of metal or plastic as they are today, but out of stiff cardboard. When Will was Lil Man's age his mother bought one for him that he used to like playing with. For hours on end he would keep turning the spindle, watch the clown pop out and laugh, then put it back inside the box and start all over again. He recalled his mother's story of buying three in one year because he kept wearing them out.

"Nice toy, Lil Man. I used to have one when I was your age."

"Yeah?" his son asked.

Will nodded. "Uh huh, and I used to play with it all the time."

"I didn't know that, daddy."

Will smiled. "That's right. In fact, Grandma bought me one too."

Lil Man's eyes lit up, letting out a big "Woooow" in amazement. Kids are always amazed at things adults deem boring, mundane. Sometimes it makes you wonder at what age do adults lose their sense of discovery? Children are great when it comes to that, but as you get older it seems your soul dies, turning into something different. It becomes so tattered and worn, cynical from years of broken promises by pushy, greedy adults. But in Lil Man's eyes, everything was interesting. Everything was cool. Getting old sucks sometimes, doesn't it?

Lil Man slid the box across the floor to his father, who took a look at the clown. His mother's words from earlier suddenly rang in his ears: "I just want you to use your gift responsibly instead of looking like a clown onstage. That's all."

"How could she call me a fucking clown?" he thought. Will looked deep into the clown's blue eyes. There were creases and slight cracks in its face that he couldn't see from the distance. Its red hair, though still full, sat clumped together, knotted, in some places. The blue suit with white polka dots had faded over the years; the hands were no longer bright white as when it was first made; instead they had begun to yellow. Still and all, it was clear that someone had taken good care of it. He put the clown back inside the box and turned it over. On the bottom the initials 'T.M.G - 1936' were carved into the cardboard.

"Must've been a former owner," Will mused. "Wanna see daddy turn the spindle?"

Lil Man nodded, watched his daddy slowly turn the spindle:

All around the Mulberry Bush

The monkey chased the weasel

The monkey stopped to pull up his sock

POP! goes the weasel

SMACK! As the clown popped out the box, Will felt a powerful, invisible force strike his face. He fell backward against the floor and immediately grabbed his nose. His hands felt wet, something streamed through his fingers. Blood.

Will kept his nose covered and stumbled into the bathroom, grabbing toilet paper to help stop the bleeding. He could feel his nose swelling up through the tissue – a pulsing, throbbing pain that pushed its way through every blood vessel in his face. How was it possible to break your nose without touching it? He didn't know what caused it, but he could swear someone hit him. But who? There wasn't anyone else in the room besides him and Lil Man.

After several minutes, the bleeding finally stopped, though the throbbing had not. Will felt as if his heart had come up from his chest and pushed its way through his nose. He dropped the bloodied paper into the toilet and looked into the mirror. What he saw truly surprised him.

His nose had turned bright red and become as round as a golf ball.

"What the fuck?" He gently touched his nose, the soreness miraculously having gone away. The harder he pressed the louder a squeaking noise had come though his nostrils.

"Christ! My fucking nose is..."

Lil Man came up from behind, holding the Jack-in-the-Box. As soon as he saw his father's face he pointed and began giggling.

"Get outta here!" Will screamed at his son, shoving him out the door. Lil Man tripped and fell, the Jack-in-the-Box flew behind him, landing near the couch. He grabbed his head and started crying. Will scooped his son off the floor and threw him over his shoulder, trying to calm him down.

"I'm sorry, Lil Man. I didn't mean to hurt you...daddy didn't mean it...shhhhhh...shhhhh...it's gonna be all right...shhhhh...I'm sorry, baby!"

Will moistened a face cloth with cold water and held it against his son's head. The compress helped ease the pain and eventually Lil Man stopped crying. His father dried his tears and kissed his son's forehead.

"Feel better?" Lil Man nodded his head. His smile quickly returned and he began pressing his father's nose over and over again. Squeak! Squeak! Squeak!

"Okay, okay – that's enough. Go sit on the couch and play with your toy!"

He patted his son on the behind and sent him on his way, then slowly looked at his nose again, examining it closely. Sure enough, it had been broken – but still he wondered how it could have done that without something hitting it.

"What happened to me? I can't go out and perform like this! I'm gonna have to cancel..."

He heard the sound of Lil Man's toy:

All around the Mulberry Bush

The monkey chased the weasel

The monkey stopped to pull up his sock

POP! goes the weasel

Will's head felt as if he were slamming it repeatedly against a brick wall. He lost his balance and fell to the ground, writhing about the floor. The pain was so fierce that he actually couldn't scream, as if he were in the middle of having a grand mal seizure. His right leg kicked the bathroom door shut as he kept his hands pressed against his head for fear it might explode, when he felt something hairy growing through his fingers. Something long, stringy and thick coursed its way around his palms and wrists until he could no longer keep his hands against his head. Will was bald and clean shaven, but within seconds he had grown a full head of red hair. His eyebrows were now long and bushy; lips became fuller and matched his red nose. His skin had turned as white as a ghost!

He clawed along the tiled floor and pushed himself against the wall, struggling to regain his balance. He could feel the bushiness of his hair and eyebrows, but it wasn't until after he managed to stand up straight where he could see what had taken place.

Will hardly recognized the man in the mirror anymore. His eyes opened wide, body trembled as he carefully touched his red hair and white skin. In a fit of rage he punched the mirror, shards flew everywhere. He cut himself on the glass and ran cold water over his fist, watching in disbelief as blood flowed through his fingers and down the drain, leaving behind pasty, leathery white skin. He took off his shirt, his denim jeans, his socks. Same thing. His entire body looked exactly the same.

"Daddy, are you okay?" Lil Man asked from behind the door.

"I'm fine, kiddo. Something broke in here, so don't come in. Stay outside and play with your toy!"

"Okay," said Lil Man, as Will began crying – not knowing what had caused all this to happen.

"What am I gonna do? I can't go onstage looking like this? I'll be a fucking joke! It's over, it's all over. I look like a...like a clown!"

Indeed he was, literally. This was exactly what his mother said he would be. Despite the money, the cars, the expensive trips, luxury hotels and the like – he had become something he was unable to explain, to understand. For as long as he could remember, being a star in the rap game was all he ever wanted to be. Nothing else mattered, and Will would sell his soul to the devil in order to make his dreams come true. Now that appeared to be the case. He was now a clown, the outward manifestation of his internal self. There was no way to explain it, and as of now, there appeared to be no way to change back to himself. Then again, perhaps this is who he really was.

"There has to be a way...a way to fix this. I can't remain a clown all my life. How did this happen to me? How..." He remembered Lil Man outside, playing with his new toy.

The Jack-in-the-Box!

Will grabbed a body towel and covered his head. And just as he was about to walk out the bathroom he heard the sound again:

All around the Mulberry Bush

The monkey chased the weasel

The monkey stopped to pull up his sock

POP! goes the weasel

Will grabbed both ankles and collapsed a second time. He pulled off both gym shoes and could see his feet swell up as if suffering from a severe edema, growing so large that they burst through his socks. Three toe nails came off of his left foot, his white skin turned purple from the sudden pressure. His feet hurt too much to stand, so he crawled toward the closed door. He barely managed to get it open and make his way back into the dressing room when Lil Man finally saw his father: red hair, lips and nose, white skin, oversized feet. The young boy was initially shocked by his father's appearance, then dropped the Box and pointed. He was laughing.

"Daddy, you're so funny!" he giggled. "Daddy's funny!"

Will reached out to his son. "Give me the Box! Give it to me!"

Lil Man picked up the Jack-in-the-Box and was about to hand it to him, when suddenly he stopped. Instead his son put his hand on the spindle. He was going to turn it.

"Don't touch that, son! Give it to daddy, please!"

Lil Man started to turn it again:

All around the Mulberry Bush

The monkey chased the weasel

The monkey stopped to pull up his sock...

"NO!" Will jumped and grabbed the Box, snatching from Lil Man. A loud SNAP rang in Will's ears, and to his dismay he saw the broken end of the spindle in Lil Man's small hand.

"Shit!" He slammed the toy on the floor, the box cracked nearly in half. The lid popped open and out came the clown, bobbing back and forth until it finally came to a stop.

Will couldn't look at it anymore. Instead he lay on his back and covered his eyes, crying. He really fucked up big time now. He broke the spindle and the box. His entire body looked like he'd been painted white. He had bright red hair, lips and a nose to match. He had a concert in less than two hours and was on the front end of a major tour. And despite his appearance, the only thing still running through his mind was how was he going to get paid looking like a clown? As usual, nothing else had mattered.

"It looks like you, daddy! Woooow!" Lil Man said, pointing at the broken box.

Will didn't budge at first until Lil Man kept bugging him. Reluctantly the dejected star sat up and glanced at the box, noting that the clown was not a clown at all, but the head of the puppet and how it was dressed looked strikingly familiar. Will picked up the broken box.

"My God...it's me!"

***

One Hour Before Show Time – Will and Moms talking via Telephone:

"Momma, where are you?" Will asked.

"I'm over at 79th and Cottage Grove getting my hair done. Why?"

"I need Felicia's cell. Do you have it on you?"

"Yes, but what's the big hurry?"

"I got a couple of acts to go on before me. I need her to pick up a new outfit."

"What's wrong? You don't like what I got for you?"

"Please, not now! Do you have her number or not?"

"Yes, yes I have it! Good grief, hold on...now where is that damn...oh here it is...ready?"

"Yeah!"

"773-537-6123...you got that?"

"Yeah, thanks!"

"Good, now what's this..."

CLICK!

***

Back to the Show!

Look at these motherfuckers out here, getting all up into this shit! I'm up on stage straight up looking like Bozo and they're lovin' every bit of it! Who would've thought I'd be spittin' lyrics and wearing a clown suit in front of thousands of fans? Not me, but then again – whatever it takes to make that paper is all I'm concerned about anyway. That and entertaining my fans, keeping them happy. Success is a must as far as I'm concerned. I could care less about the rest.

After a good hour I finally took my first break. My manager went crazy when I stepped off stage and changed into a new clown suit. Not crazy in a bad way. He was deep into it, calling me 'one smart nigga' in between phone calls to promoters across the country, trying to line up more gigs. He was thinkin' we could bump up this tour, make it international. Spain, Australia, the UK. Shit, this nigga's taking me places I ain't never been before, and I've been doing my thing for over a decade! And after all this is done all I need to do is chill out and watch the loot roll in. I can buy Moms a bigger house! I can put more money away for Lil Man and have everything covered for Angie. She's gonna be a doctor no matter what!

As for me, I'm gonna keep owning this crowd, keep my edge, keep Sabo and me paid, keep this game going. See, at first I was thinking if I get the Jack-in-the-Box fixed I could turn the spindle backwards and return back to normal. Felicia has it now and said she would find someone to repair it. Make it look like brand new. But now I'm thinking – maybe I don't wanna change back to 'Me' just yet. Maybe I should ride this clown-thing out for a while, see how it works out. If the crowd is going nuts over this now, you wait until these lyrics hit the stores. This is gonna be the coldest shit on the streets! Niggas are gonna eat it up, no doubt. And all my harshest critics are gonna talk, I know – but at the end of the day they know what they've gotta do: follow the leader, just like Eric B and Rakim said years ago.

Look, I know I've got some making up to do with Moms. Right after my manager broke the news about the extended tour she walked away from me, leaving the auditorium. I know I pissed her off. I know I'm wrong, that I look like a freak out there. I know this. But I've got a lot of pressure, see what I'm saying? I've gotta keep money coming in. I'm the pied piper of this rap game! I'm a star, baby! Gotta keep it moving, no matter what. Still, it ain't gonna be easy; Moms can be pretty stubborn when she wants to be, but eventually she'll see things my way. Tomorrow I'll have Felicia go to a Lexus dealer and pick something out for her. 'Bout time for her to get a new ride, anyway. She'll forgive me. She always does.

If anyone would cause me to change my ways it would be Lil Man. Right now it's cool because he's just a kid. Kids love clowns. Besides, kids love their parents unconditionally anyway, right? See I've thought all this out. What I'll do is keep this thing going for a while, then re-evaluate. I figure when he gets older he'll ask me about why I dressed up like a clown during my rap days, and I'll sit down and point to his trust fund and his first car and the college tuition I paid for and say: son, daddy had to go make that money so he could provide for his family. And when I'm done telling him, he's gonna understand and love his Pops even more.

Quite honestly, it doesn't bother me that I'm a clown. At the very least I know who I am on the inside, and that's all that matters. Off stage I'm William Robinson, but on stage I'm known as 'Big Will'. I'm an entertainer. This is what I do for a living. This is how I make people happy. This is how I get paid. And I'm gonna keep on making these hits, making people get off their feet and dance to my music, no matter what it takes.

Know what I'm sayin'?

CANDLES

April 11, 2010. My 40th Birthday.

Go ahead, Michael! Blow them out! Blow them out!

That's how my dream always began. The searing heat nearly melting my skin, the light from the candles on my birthday cake seemed bright enough to burn down this entire restaurant, meanwhile the only thing I'm mulling over is the precise method in which I'm going to kill Gordon later on tonight when we get home. This is usually how the dream starts; only now it isn't a dream at all. It's actually happening. I'm finally turning forty years old, the illustrious age in which life is supposed to begin. My friends are standing around me, almost exactly as they were in my unconscious mind during the course of the past week, waiting patiently for the completion of my wish and the ceremonial blowing out of the candles. And to think, I'm one of few people I know of who actually wants to celebrate this day in such fashion - minus all these damn candles, of course.

It's true. I wanted a birthday party, but after several threats from my partner of thirteen years, I repeatedly begged him not to put this many candles on my cake. One would be sufficient, or even the number "40" would've been acceptable. What did he do? He did exactly what I asked him not to, God bless him! So here I am, in one of my favorite restaurants on the north side, my face boiling because it looks like someone set the place on fire and I can't help but smile, thinking I'm going to need an extinguisher to put these candles out.

"Go 'head, Gertie - just put your lips together and blow," said Teddy, my ex-boyfriend from long ago. That's a whole other story, trust me.

"Honey, if he can blow that hard I'm giving him my phone number," Chris joked. Of course everyone laughed. I have to admit, that was a good one.

I guess I should learn to ease up, live a little. I always have been sort of a tight ass, even after all the years of living with Gordon. He was the funny one of the two of us, and it was because of him that I have grown up, so to speak. Boy I'm a lucky guy! I recall years back when we first met. It was a cliché moment, but I happened to be in a restaurant called The Roxbury over on East Ohio Street, not far from Water Tower Place. A few friends and I were hanging out and about to leave for the movies when this guy walked in and sat down across from me. Our eyes met and we both smiled, though I was fairly shy back in those days. I knew he was still looking at me, even as he ordered his meal from the waitress.

Not long before that moment, Teddy and I had broken up, but remained friends. Sometimes things work out better that way. Teddy liked to party, party, party. Me? Even back then I was somewhat of a homebody. Why pay eight bucks for a margarita when I made the best one in all of Chicago right at home? Besides – too much nonsense happens late at night, but I digress. Anyway, Teddy was with me that night – me, Chris, Teddy and Randall – and he caught this nice looking guy staring at me and nudged me repeatedly under the table. I stepped on his foot so he would knock it off, but he only did it right back to me, nodding his head in this guy's direction. I rolled my eyes at him.

We were about to leave when Teddy shoved me back in my seat.

"Uh uh, Gertie - you stay here and have another drink. I'll call you tomorrow," he said. Teddy loved naming his male friends after famous women, so he deemed it apropos to call me Gertie, short for Gertrude Stein, because I'm a writer. And as he walked by Gordon's table he said: "his name is Michael and he's available, so go say hi." I could have killed him for that, but what else could I say? My name was Michael, and yes, I was available, but Teddy knew me well. Had he not done that I would have walked right on by without saying a word, so I sucked up as much nerve as I could and took a seat across from this nicely groomed, conservatively dressed man.

"Name's Michael Gannon," I said.

"So I've heard," said the man. "I'm Gordon Jarrett..."

"...pleasure to...meet...you..." we awkwardly said together, shaking hands.

I grinned at him like the Cheshire Cat from Alice in Wonderland. Ironically, both Gordon and Teddy said the same exact thing about me when we first met: "you have great teeth." "Why thank you," I said. "I've got my father's teeth." Funny how something like that could make a difference, right?

I had that same grin on me right now in front the dinner table. For a brief moment, I took the time to look around at my smiling friends; friends who for many years had told me how special I was and how much I meant to their lives. I failed to see how any of that was possible, me being the kind of person who doesn't get caught up in personal accolades. But one thing I always did was value the friendships I'd made over the years. I was always one to think of someone whom I hadn't seen in a long time. At any given moment an old friend would come to mind and I'd raid my closet looking for any address book that had their number. We'd rekindle the special moments from our lives and continue forward with new and exciting adventures. Those were always the best kinds of friendships, in my opinion. You could be out of touch with someone for years, but once the connection has been refreshed, you were back where you left off – sharing, laughing, being you all over again. I suppose this is why Gordon insisted in overdoing the birthday cake with all these damn candles, or Chris' flaming remark about getting my phone number, or Teddy's insistence on me talking to this wonderful man to my right, who subsequently became my partner. The point is they care. They care enough to be here on my special day, and I care for them simply because they're here with me.

Sometimes we forget these things. On occasion I'd get so bogged down with nonsense that I'm unable to see the forest for the trees. Life does that, you know?

But if we're the right kind of people, the kind that try to remain open to what's going on around us, those special moments arrive when we least expect it, and sometimes the person who brings the knowledge could literally walk in and out of our lives within minutes. I had an experience like that once, not long ago. It happened with an old man; a strange looking old man that I met on the train over a week ago, who helped me to remember the importance of friendship, commitment and respect.

My grandmother used to tell me that sometimes it takes a stranger to put things back in perspective. Before a few weeks ago, I never would've believed her. Who would think someone who doesn't know you could see inside your heart and give it to you straight? Certainly not me, but all of that changed a week ago as I boarded the Red Line train heading for downtown. March 27th was the day; seven AM was the time.

A time for change.

***

March 27, 2010. Jarvis Red Line Stop. 6:57 AM. Chicago, Illinois.

I was in a hurry that day. From our apartment on North Greenview Avenue I could hear the train coming from Howard, so I high tailed it out the front door and ran full speed past Dora's Café, past Luigi's Italian Kitchen, past Ned - the beggar guy from around the way that always seemed to have decent clothes on despite being "homeless."

"No time today, Ned," I huffed, running up the staircase two-at-a-time. Just as I made it to the train platform the doors had opened.

"This...is... Jarvis! The next stop ...is...Morse!... (DING DONG!)...doors closing!" said the recorded voice, as if everyone were on pins and needles to hear the name of the next station.

I like our neighborhood. I've lived here for almost eleven years and I've seen it go through tremendous change. Rogers Park used to be a dump. Broken glass, trash, street gangs, boarded up storefronts and rusted-out cars that hadn't moved for weeks was what I lived around back then, but sometime around the mid-Nineties it started to come up. More people with money came into the area, bought the properties for dirt cheap and fixed them up. The storefronts reopened. Chic coffee shops, like Dora's Café, sprouted up. More police and local politicians moved into the area. Gays and lesbians, looking to get away from the noise in Lakeview, sought refuge here. It was an amazing time to buy, and once Gordon and I bought the place, we were able to pay off an $80k mortgage in ten years. There were lots of sacrifices on our part – few vacations, conservative spending habits, etc. – but it truly was worth it. Now we have it all – a nice apartment owned free and clear, a beautiful neighborhood that was steps away from the Lake, great places to eat and quaint theaters to catch a movie. Believe it or not, Ned was the only thing remaining of Rogers Park's inglorious past. Everyone knew him, and though he was harmless, we always wondered where he was from. Rumor has it that he actually isn't homeless, but is well off and owns several houses in the area. While I didn't know for certain, I noticed he was always clean-shaven and had better than average clothes despite being "homeless." Oh well. Ned's a good guy.

Today I had a meeting with my agent downtown, so I thought I'd try to get to The Loop a little early and have a coffee in Millennium Park. The weather was nice and the Crown Fountain would be flowing for the tourists. Rich, my agent, set up an appointment with someone from Penguin Books who wanted to discuss a three-book deal, so I thought it imperative that I be there. I've done well with smaller publishers and have gained a tremendous following, but my last book, Time and Turmoil, put me on the map. The reviews were tremendous and I've been doing readings, both large and small, all across the country. I've been blessed indeed.

Instead of being happy with my recent success, I was a bit in the dumps about turning forty. The nightmares I'd been having were crazy. Things seemed different to me now, even though my birthday was a week away. Lately I've found it hard listening to the same music that I had just a few years ago. While in my twenties I used to watch Russell Simmons' Def Comedy Jam, but after buying a DVD with the all-time greatest shows, I found them repulsive and gave them away to my friend Barry, who seems unwilling (or incapable) of growing up. I decided to go visit my old neighborhood on the South Side, but found it smaller and narrower than I ever had before. Poor Gordon! For weeks he's listened to my neurotic babble, until one day he couldn't take it anymore and said: "You know what? There's a whole cemetery full of people who would love to have one more birthday!"

With that he stormed out of the room, leaving me behind, speechless. That was the end of my 'forty-year-old-woe-is-me' conversations with him. The sad part was even after his comments I still hadn't a clue, so for days I sat quietly, brooding on my own just like I am at this moment. I stared outside the window, the lovely campus of Loyola University passing me by with just a quick glimpse of Lake Michigan peeking in between Tanner Hall and Madonna Della Strata Chapel, ensconced in my own foolishness like some pouting kid. The El provided a front row seat to a lovely sunrise that I couldn't see due to apartment buildings that flew by my window. I had a blues that was deeper than any John Lee Hooker song, and it was getting worse every day.

"This...is... Granville! The next stop ...is...Thorndale!... (DING DONG!)...doors closing!"

There was a 'drag-step' sound that neared my seat. My head was down and I could see a pair of worn black leather shoes in front of me, along with three full white plastic bags. I looked up and saw an elderly African-American man with sullen brown eyes and a grisly looking beard. His dress was conservative, neat. He wore a long sleeve white oxford shirt and black slacks. On his head was a grey fedora with a black band that stretched around the outside. He wore no rings or jewelry, though he did have a silver Swiss Army watch around his left wrist.

His demeanor was pleasant and he smiled at me politely. It was then I noticed he and I were the only ones on the train. Typical for this time of day, so I didn't find it strange.

I nodded at the man. "Morning," I said.

His smile had widened. Despite his appearance his teeth actually looked in better shape than mine. Take THAT, Gordon and Teddy!

"Good morning young man. Fine day, isn't it?" the Old Man asked.

"Yeah, I suppose so," I replied, still in my ridiculous funk.

The Old Man looked at me suspiciously. "That wasn't very convincing. A young guy like you? Unable to appreciate such a nice day? Sounds like trouble to me."

I laughed. "I think you're right. In fact, I know you're right."

"Something wrong? Care to tell an old man your trouble?"

For some reason I didn't mind. I had no idea who this man was, but he seemed nice enough. What's the harm in opening up a little to a complete stranger?

"I'm turning forty in a few days," I said with doom and dread in my voice. The Old Man's eyes brightened at my revelation.

"Well congratulations, young man. Turning forty is a big deal, you know."

I shrugged. "Nah, a pain in the ass is more like it to me. I'm like in the middle – too old to go to a club, not old enough to sit in a rocking chair. Sounds bad, but it's true."

The Old Man belted out a hearty laugh. His head went back, Adam's apple bouncing up and down like a rubber ball. I suppose if I were his age looking at some dour whippersnapper like me I'd laugh too. I couldn't help it though. This was an age that I never expected to see, despite my steady diet of green tea and steamed broccoli each week.

"What in the world makes you say such a thing? You look in great shape to me. You know what they say – if you have your health, you have everything."

"I know. Sorry – not a nice way to start a conversation. Name's Michael," I replied, extending my hand. The Old Man had quite a grip.

"Nice to meet you. Now what's with this age problem of yours? I get concerned when I hear youngun's like you start talking that way."

"Oh it's nothing really. Me being ridiculous is all."

"Son, it's not nice to lie to a senior citizen. They got rules against that kind of thing, you know."

I laughed, held up my hands. "Sorry. It's been an interesting week, to say the least. It's funny; I've been looking forward to it and dreading it at the same time. Guess I'm in 'dread' mode right now."

The Old Man said: "Dread is a sympathetic antipathy and an antipathetic sympathy."

"Kierkegaard?" I asked.

He nodded. "Very good, but you're a writer, so I would expect you to know that."

"How'd you know?"

"Know what?" he asked.

"You're right – I AM a writer, but how did you know?"

He tapped the middle of his forehead. "Can't you tell, young man? I've got a third eye – right here. See? It knows all."

He slid back into his seat, smirked. "Besides, I read 'Time and Turmoil'. Great book. Nice picture of you on the inside cover."

"You're funny," I replied.

"Mr. Gannon, when you get to be my age you can do all sorts of fun things. Comes with the territory. Mind if I join you?"

He gestured to the seat next to me; I nodded, clearing off a left behind copy of today's Chicago Sun-Times.

"You say you're back and forth about your age. I can understand why. I was that age myself. Remember it well. My father told me a long time ago that life began at forty, and he was right. He didn't mean you were suddenly footloose and fancy free, but that you were finally coming into your own, hitting your prime."

"I get that, but it doesn't feel right. I can't explain it."

"What's not to feel right about? It's your age, your time. It's all yours to do as you wish."

"I know, but it reminds me of my dad. He passed on Christmas Day. I was only four."

"Oh I'm sorry," he replied.

"Yeah, thanks. Freak accident. He was putting together a train set for me and dropped the milk that I left for "Santa" just as the electrical current hit the tracks. Sometimes I think if I hadn't left that milk or asked for the train set he would still be alive."

The Old Man sat forward in his seat. "Young man, it wasn't your fault. Like you said, it was a freak accident. Besides, what's this got to do with turning forty?"

I took a deep breath. "My dad was forty when he died."

The Old Man sighed, his face turned somber. He momentarily turned away, staring out the window next to me just as the train hit a turn and rattled violently.

"Ah, now I understand. And here you are, busy carrying this around like dead weight."

I nodded. "I've got someone special in my life, a great career and lots of friends and I sometimes wonder if I deserve any of it."

"Would any of these people agree with you?"

"No – they'd think I was being stupid."

"So would I," he replied.

"You would?"

"Oh yes."

The train shook again as we left Addison Street; strangely enough no one had come aboard since I left Jarvis. This kindly old man listened to me with great patience while I kept rattling on and on about myself. I was glad that he did – there was so much on my mind and I had to get it out to someone, though Gordon should be the one to hear all of this.

"I've been having these weird dreams, you know? I'm at my birthday party and just as I'm about to blow out the candles something crazy always happens. Once the fire actually grew and burned down the restaurant; another time the sprinklers were set off.

70

Funny thing was it was only me that seemed to realize what was going on. Very strange."

"Well, that's the mind of a writer. Imaginative, thinking of the craziest scenarios."

Interesting assessment. I agreed.

He paused, asked: "May I share something with you?"

"Please."

"I have a son just like you. Smart. Creative. Funny. He showed me early on how much talent he had, and I did everything I could to help nurture that. So did his mother. We tried to be upstanding parents for our son, teach him the right things so he would lead a good life on his own someday. Now he's grown up and successful, but doubts himself, worries about things way too much."

I felt a nudge from the Old Man's bony elbow. "You're way too hard on yourself, Michael. You didn't cause your daddy's death, ya hear?"

I gave a conciliatory nod, unconvinced by his words. Until now I had never spoken to anyone about this – not even to Gordon. Honestly I should be ashamed of myself. If there was anyone in the world that I should share this with, it was him. But it all gets back to how I've always been – quiet, reserved, even boring at times. I really need to get over it.

"This...is...Clark and Division! This is a Red Line train to 95th Street! Doors open on the left!"

The Old Man stared out the window, pointed. "I get off on Chicago Avenue. If you have time, how 'bout coming over to my store for a cup of coffee and some of my homemade scones? You're missing out if you don't."

I laughed. Besides, who could pass up good conversation over homemade scones?

"Okay, let's go!"

***

We got off the Red Line, headed west on Chicago Avenue and made a right on Dearborn. Back in the day this used to be one of my favorite hangout spots because of the old Chestnut Station Theater that was on the corner. One of the first movies I ever saw there, or shall I say PAID to see, was *Beat Street*, a movie about breakdancing, popping and locking, set in New York City. I emphasized the word PAID because just before the credits rolled me and a few friends snuck out across the corridor and went into another theater to see *Breakin'*, another popular film about breakers from LA. One of my friends met us after Beat Street had already started, so his dumb ass kept going from theater to theater so he could see what he missed. Eventually one of the security guards caught on and threw him out. Not only did Robert not see all of Beat Street but he also missed the rest of Breakin'. He watched half of two different movies and threw four dollars down the drain.

Four dollars? Good Lord, I'm getting old.

I walked to the corner and looked at what was now a Jewish Synagogue, searching the area for any sign of the old theater, but there was nothing left. The building had been razed back in '99 and the temple was built from the ground up. Sad. This used to be such a fun place to hang out, but when the crack era hit it took away the grand appeal of the theater, bringing a dangerous element to the neighborhood. Chestnut Station stopped showing first rate shows and went to movies with B-film stars like Charles Bronson and Chuck Norris, thugs from the nearby projects started coming around starting trouble, selling dope and harassing patrons until decent folks stopped coming around. Eventually the worst had happened; someone was murdered right in front of the double glass doors leading to the theater lobby. Two weeks after that the Chestnut had shut down for good. Rumors flew around that it was going to reopen, but it never did. Instead it sat empty for nearly two years until members of the Jewish Community bought the land and tore away any reminder of the old theater. Thugs stopped coming around and the block experienced a terrific renaissance, but still it feels different. God, I miss those days.

I had been standing off on my own for a while, so much to the point where I didn't realize the Old Man was standing next to me.

"Thinking of the old Chestnut?" he asked.

I nodded, said: "Lots of great times in this neighborhood, 'til crack came along."

"Well, it was rough, that's for sure 'nuf. But things have been good around here for a while now. I don't see it changin' again anytime soon. C'mon – let's get you some coffee."

The Old Man led me over to his storefront which was two doors down from the temple. It was early still, so few people were out and about. Funny but I didn't recall seeing anyone on Dearborn since we turned from Chicago Avenue. Oh well, perhaps it was my imagination. This neighborhood always was like some secluded alcove, hidden away from the rest of the world. It had always been that way, I suppose.

He opened a huge master lock and raised the security gate, then unlocked the front door – "The Dhamira Curio and Gift Shop" etched on the glass in Old English font. On my way in I checked the door, the two display windows – only a sign that said "OPEN" and "CLOSED" was up front. There were no days and times of operation listed anywhere. Strange.

"You really should put more information in your window, Sir. People won't know when to find you."

He turned, laughed at me: "Young man, people find me, I don't find them. When I'm here I usually have a guest, or someone will come in who has the uncontrollable urge to buy and can't explain it!"

I laughed. "I see. Must be your magnetic personality at work, eh?"

"Something like that, yes. And now – coffee and scones."

I followed the Old Man through his store. The further down the center aisle I went, the more the walls were closing in on me, as if I were in the belly of some huge monstrosity that had eaten me whole. To my right were all kinds of party favors: streamers, birthday hats, costumes, signs, paper napkins. Against the far wall was a huge collection of balloons, especially ones with a "smiley-face" that were in a variety of colors.   To the left there were all kinds of odd looking items for sale: dream catchers, ceramic kittens, 'ships in bottles', hand-knitted throw pillows, designer pottery and antique touchier lamps. The place looked old, though there was a certain charm to it that I couldn't put my finger on. For some reason everything looked like it had already belonged to someone else, not traded in or donated, but bought – as if the item had been on layaway, waiting for a specific person to come pick it up. Sounds strange, I know, but something clearly felt a bit off kilter. The Old Man himself seemed a bit off kilter for that matter.

"See anything you like?" he asked, as I stared at something on one of his shelves.

"Is this an old drinking bird? The one that bobs up and down in a glass of water?"

I carefully picked up the glass bird and examined it closely, running my finger along its yellow beak and black top hat. My folks bought me one of these when I was little. I used to sit for hours and wonder how it was able to do that. To this day I remember dad saying it had something to do with converting heat energy, or something like that. To be honest, I didn't care. I was just surprised that it could duck its head in the water and pop up and rock, like an old lady in a chair.

The Old Man stood next to me, smiling at the bird. "That's it, alright. They don't make toys like these anymore. It's always nice when I run across something like this, all the nostalgia that comes with it."

I agreed wholeheartedly. "No doubt. I had one of these years ago. Mom and Dad bought this as a birthday gift when I was four and marked my initials on the left foot in case it got lost. My folks had a party for me that day; a few hours later the bird turned up missing."

The Old Man sighed. "Someone took it? One of your friends, maybe?"

"Think so. But the person who DID take it never came clean. I was pretty upset; my father offered to buy me another one, but I refused. "Mr. Storkey" was the only one I wanted. "

The Old Man stifled a laugh. "Mr. Storkey, huh?"

"Yep, sorry. That about the best one could do at age four."

Both men laughed. "Okay, tell you what – lets enjoy the coffee and scones and I'll wrap Mr. Storkey up for you as a birthday gift. On the house."

"Oh no, I couldn't do that. I will take him, though. How much?"

The Old Man flatly refused. "Under no circumstances, young man. Consider it a first toast to a long friendship. Okay?"

"Alright, then, to a long friendship," I said a few minutes later as we raised our coffee mugs before sampling The Old Man's delicious blueberry streusel scones and fresh percolated coffee. He was right about one thing: these were the best scones I had ever tasted in my life, not hard or bland like some I've sampled over the years. These were bursting with juicy blueberries with a tasty streusel topping that gave them a delightful crunch, the crisp crust and rich buttery flavor had an aftertaste that was absolutely sinful. I dare say these rivaled my mother's, God bless her. Of course I would never tell her such a thing, for she'd never speak to me again, but I couldn't help but be reminded of momma with each bite. Looks can be deceiving, but one thing was crystal clear - this Old Man could bake.

"Absolutely wonderful," I said, finishing the last bite. I wiped my hands on a paper towel and washed down the remnants with coffee, also quite delightful.

"Where did you get this coffee? Starbucks?"

"Oh heavens no, young man. I bought it at a Middle Eastern store on Foster and Sheridan in Uptown called Kalil's Bakery and Grocery. Great place. Friendly people. You should go there sometime."

"I will. This really is good coffee. I don't drink it much. My partner Gordon, however, practically needs an IV drip to pump it in. Totally addicted to the stuff."

"I see. And how long have the two of you been together?" he asked.

"Thirteen years, God bless him. I'm very lucky."

"That's all that a father could ever ask for his son...that you're happy, I mean. You've lived a great life with so much more to do, and I'm very proud of you."

Admittedly I was quite touched by the sentiment. Sometimes I feel a bit unsteady, not certain of the right way to go. But there's a lot to be proud of, and my birthday should be a moment that I take for me and give thanks. I'm far from perfect, but I'm even further from being nobody.

The Old Man collected our plates, put them in the sink and washed them. "I'm sorry, but I'm going to have to open the shop soon. I have a woman coming by who wants to buy an antique Jack-in-the-Box at 8:30 and she's in a hurry."

I rose from the table. "Oh no problem. I should be going myself. I've got a meeting with my agent later this morning and I don't want to be late."

"Oh? What's it about?" he asked as he escorted me back into the store. We made our way down the center aisle; the clichéd 'light at the end of the tunnel' became larger the closer we came to the front register.

"Well, I'm meeting with a representative from Penguin Books about a possible three-book deal. I'm keeping my hands crossed. This could set me up for life if I do it right."

He shook my hand, saying: "Congratulations Son. I'm sure you'll do well. Oh...before I forget! Let me wrap up that gift for you. I'll be back in a minute."

He scurried back into the darkness, swallowed up in the boughs of this unusual store, where shortly thereafter I could hear the sound of tape and scissors and other muffled sounds, similar to something being wrapped. A few moments later, the Old Man returned with a small box and a greeting card with my name on it. With a huge smile on his face, he presented my early birthday gift to me, proud as could be. I was truly flattered, never having hit it off so well and so quickly before. If this was any indication of how the rest of my day (and my life would be, for that matter), I'm a lucky man.

"Thank you, uh...you know what?...I feel ridiculous in saying this, but I didn't catch your name."

He laughed. "That's because I never threw it. Name's Thomas." We shook hands as if we had just met, but that's not the truth at all. We've met, alright – just not in this life. Among his other quirks, Teddy believes in Tarot Cards and reincarnation and all that other crap, going around saying how strangers that we become close almost instantly were friends and lovers from our past lives who recognize each other by spirit, not by face. Grandma used to say the same thing, though I didn't believe her either.

"Pleasure to meet you, Thomas. You already know me."

He nodded. "Yes indeed, I do. By the way, here's a box of candles for your birthday cake. Can't have a cake without candles, right?"

"Thanks, and you're right. Candles are a must. Well, I have to get going. My meeting is at 9:30 and I don't want to be late."

"Yes sir. Go ahead and best of luck to you, young man. It really has been a pleasure."

"Yes it has. I hope to do it again someday." I really meant that.

"Uh huh. Same here. We'll see."

I grabbed my package and bid Thomas farewell, and as I was leaving the store an older black woman walked in, did a double-take and touched my shoulder. She looked at me as if she were trying to figure me out. Trust me, others have tried and weren't successful.

"Excuse me, sir. Are you Michael Gannon?"

Or perhaps they WERE successful. "Why yes, I am. How did you know?"

"Are you kidding me? I have your books, and I really love *Time and Turmoil.* Wonderful! I can't wait to read more of your work."

"Why thank you, Miss..."

"Robinson...Anna Mae Robinson. And if you don't mind, can you autograph my book? I have it here in my bag."

"Of course, please."

Anna reached in her purse and pulled out her copy of my book, which I signed in the back where my picture was located. I never did like signing a book in the front like most writers. That's one of the things I've always believed in – doing things different from others, which I think has led to more personal success in the long run. Signing under my picture gives it a more personal touch; whenever someone looks at the rear of the book I want them to remember this moment, even if I happen to forget, which was often the case. My agent told me once we started doing book tours that 'the nicer I am at the very beginning, the greater the chance I retain that person as a reader – one that will identify with me as well as my characters better'. I couldn't agree more. Besides, if there's one thing I'll always remember about my father – it was his ability to remain humble. Always humble. Always caring. Always loving. That's what I miss most about him.

"There you go. I'm glad you enjoyed it. I've got a new one coming out soon, so be sure to look out for it, okay?"

Miss Robinson smiled at me. "Thank you, sir. I have a son of my own – talented just like you. And I'm keeping my eye on the both of you, so watch it!"

She smiled, shook my hand. "I'll be sure to look for your next book. Take care, and thank you."

I watched as she walked by me and into the store, checked my watch and started for the train when I realized I had her pen. I made my way back to the store, but found it boarded up with a sign that read: For Rent. Call 773-779-8383. I strained to see through the dusty boards and mud-caked windows, but there was nothing inside but papers and broken furniture across the floor. The walls were a faded green with a series of dirt-outlined rectangles from paintings that had been removed from the walls. Parts of the checkered floor tiles had cracked and were scattered about the area. It looked as if no one had been in this store for years.

"What the hell?" I thought, looking at the package Thomas had given to me, when it hit me – Thomas was also my father's name. The Old Man's words echoed in my mind:

"I have a son just like you. Smart. Creative. Funny. He showed me early on how much talent he had, and I did everything I could to help nurture that. So did his mother."

"You're way too hard on yourself, Michael. You didn't cause your daddy's death, ya hear?"

"That's all that a father could ever ask for his son... I'm very proud of you."

I took a seat on a nearby brownstone and opened the box,

carefully removing the glass stork out of the paper wrapping. There were a few scratches around its legs and the color was had faded, but it was in pretty good condition. I stared at the stork, thinking of my earlier conversation with Thomas: *"I had one of these years ago. Dad bought this as a birthday gift when I was four and marked my initials on the left foot in case it got lost."*

I turned over the stork and checking under its left foot, where the initials 'MTG' had been written by my father with a gold-colored galaxy medium-point marker. *Mr. Storkey!* Once lost but now found after all of these years.

At that moment I closed my eyes, imagining I was back at my fourth birthday when my mother and father sat at our kitchen table, watching me as I opened Mr. Storkey for the first time. My birthday celebration to take place later on that day; friends were coming for ice cream and cake and cookies and hot dogs and chips and music and fun. I thought of how Mr. Storkey never left my hand until it was time for me to swing at the Spider-Man piñata Dad had set up in the backyard. I remember the moment I had broken through, how my friends rushed me when the Now-Laters, metal tops, arm buzzers, Jolly Rancher candies and Charms Blow Pops came crashing down – everyone trying to cram whatever they could into their pockets before it was all gone.

I remember when I opened my gifts and the other kids, especially Tommy Daniels, were in awe of my Weebles Haunted House and my Playskool Sit 'N Spin and wanted to try it out on their own. Tommy Daniels and I nearly got into an argument over how long he should play with my toys, but my father took me aside and reminded me of the importance of sharing – something I remember to this very day. I remember Tommy's mother having to pull him away from the Sit 'N Spin, despite his teary protests. And once everyone had gone home, I remember how my parents helped me search for Mr. Storkey later on; how he turned up missing, never to be found again. Mom and Dad sat with me as I cried myself to sleep on my birthday, dejected that my favorite toy was gone. They offered to buy me another one, but I refused, saying there was only one Mr. Storkey. I insisted they not get me another one, and they respected my wishes. Even back then I was rather bull-headed; my mother often said I was born under a wrong sign – that I should have been a Taurus. For years I denied that, but eventually agreed with her. I was bull-headed. Still am to this day.

And I opened my eyes, the sun brightly shining on this mild June morning, the REAL Mr. Storkey in my hands, the day (and my whole life) in front of me where good things were bound to happen; fully aware of how blessed I am, no longer regretful about approaching a pivotal moment in my life. In fact, I embraced it right at that moment because besides Gordon and my friends, I had received a gift that meant more to me than anything else in the world. It was a beautiful gift, one that I would forever cherish no matter the circumstance.

I understood the meaning of a father's love.

***

April 11, 2010. The Big Day.
"So are you gonna blow them out, or what?"
"Quick, honey, before the fire department gets here!"
So, once again, here I am in front of this bonfire, my friends

82

ready to clap on my behalf and my partner holding my hand, giving me a tight squeeze. I took a moment to look at him, grateful that he actually cared enough about me to go through such trouble.

This is how I've always believed our lives should roll: groups of friends who are there for us, brought together by a solid foundation built on love, mutual respect and admiration, and a significant other who wants nothing more but to share our highs and lows together, side by side, hand in hand, taking on the world together. That's what I now have. That's what I've been blessed with. That's something my father, who had the chance to see me as the man I am now, had always wanted for me.

He was right. I've been too hard on myself and it's time to let go.

Gordon nudged my shoulder. "Did you make a wish?"

I nodded and leaned closer to my cake, attempting to blow out the candles, but after two tries they continued to re-light. I chuckled, realizing I'd been had by my own father. As I gave it another try, my friends took the can of Silly String they had been hiding behind their backs and fired, covering my face and head with an assortment of colors. The candles were finally out. My friends were laughing with glee. Gordon gave me a tender hug and kiss. From underneath the mound of foamy substance, I flashed all of them my father's smile, thankful to God for having them in my life.

And somewhere out there, safely within the realm of his odd store, was Thomas, my dad, standing as tall and as proud as could be.

DVD's

12:33 am

Well, it looks like it's going to be another sleep-deprived evening for me. Figures. They all began the same way: exhausted from long hours of working on a new novel in front of my laptop, a single-malt scotch after dinner, watching some mindless garbage on my Sony flat-screen, brushing and flossing my teeth for the third time today, a Xanax to help me relax before bed. I crack open a book, only to pass out around nine-thirty with my reading light still shining in my face. During the little sleep I get, nightmares from my dubious past fill my head as ominous shadows fall around me like the dusk.

Then I wake up alone. My head throbs from the combination of prescription medication and cheap booze while the light screams at me like a hungry infant. One flick of the switch and my entire world swallows me into solitude with six long hours of darkness to keep me company. The shadows that hover around my bed leer at me like an angry mob ready to attack. I am defenseless against them, separated only by my precious one-thousand thread count Egyptian cotton sheets and my mother's burnt orange quilt, one of probably a hundred that she made during the course of her eighty-three years of life.

This is all that I have to comfort me at night. I have always believed that someday these obscurities would not only surround me, but take me against my will to wherever they hide during the day, removing me completely from this sham of a life that I had willingly stolen from a fellow writer years ago. What made my crime worse was it wasn't an arbitrary person whose ideas I had confiscated as my own, but someone that I once called my friend.

His name was Nelson Ade.

***

1:27 am

Funny how Nelson's name has crept through my head more and more these days. Back when I was actually sleeping like the rest of the world, he had been an afterthought; a mere speed bump along my road to literary success. He and I were best friends in high school and had applied to the same colleges. Upon our acceptance to the University of Chicago, we chose English Literature as our major, though he also minored in French, which he had excelled in all through high school. During our first semester we discovered a common love of writing stories, so with the University's permission, he and I founded *The Washington Square Society*, a writer's group that has grown leaps and bounds since our undergraduate days. Every year my foundation gives scholarships to aspiring writers, some of whom have gone on to have successful literary careers in their own right.

I wish I could take all the credit for Washington Square's success, but that wouldn't be true, for it was really Nelson's idea. Once we discovered some of our fellow students wanted to meet after class or during breaks and recite their prose, Nelson came up with the idea to make it official. I didn't really care until he told me we could be the group's founding duo and make all the rules, which he mostly did. Even with the group going strong and Rosenwald Hall being the spot to exercise your literary "juices", the only person among us that I was in awe of was Nelson. His ideas were tremendous, and the brilliant part was he claimed to have never written any of them down. They were all inside his head – raw and undeveloped – until one Friday night, while in the middle of several shots of scotch in our dorm room, I had decided to video tape our conversation without his knowledge. Nelson rattled out nearly twenty different story ideas, complete with character descriptions, setting and mood. He even mentioned where the inspirations for these pieces had come from, completely unaware of what I was up to. I nearly had enough material to last me my entire career, and coupled with the fact he became a raging alcoholic during and after our years at the University, there was nothing to stop me from using his ideas.

At my absolute lowest, I remember searching our dorm for anything that would prove he lied to me about not having written any of these marvelous ideas of his. Even when he invited me to stay with his family during breaks or vacations at their summer home in Lake Geneva or overnight visits at their sprawling mansion in Highland Park, I would always check through every inch of the place and find nothing. Nelson churned out piece after piece and won several literary awards while in school with ideas that were fully developed exclusively inside his mind. So before he could do any more, I started working away on his later ideas. I figured out his pattern. The way he had written his pieces was the exact order in which he said on tape, so I simply began from his last piece and went backwards, working quickly so I could submit ahead of him. I knew all the journals where he had sent his work and initially figured once I'd gotten enough recognition I could work on some of my own material. Instead, I kept going and used every idea that I could until the fateful day when my treachery had caught up with me. But without any proof, Nelson had no grounds to sue; he knew that. And on Christmas Day 1994, at his parents' home, I made sure he understood that particular fact.

That was the last day he and I had ever spoken. Nelson drank himself into one dreadful stupor after another. His life and work was never the same, meanwhile I had toured the world doing lectures and interviews and book signings. Some of my books had been adapted into screenplays for film and television. In 2003 I had won a National Book Award for *The Dreadful Days of Diablo Dolenz*, by far my greatest achievement. Coincidentally, it was the last of Nelson's unpublished works of art as well as the beginning of some very mixed reviews for my original ideas until I had regained my footing with *Lux ex Tenebris*, which became a world-wide sensation. It was a cross-genre piece, more action-packed than the dramatic pieces I'd written before, but a well-told story that remained on the New York Times Best Seller List for almost a year. Thanks to my agent, I had recently secured a deal to write the screenplay, which I insisted on doing before agreeing to sell the film rights. I was lucky; had the novel not been as successful as it was, I doubt if I could have made that happen. And I practically named my own price.

All of this had been possible because of what I did to Nelson long ago. No, he didn't actually write the pieces for me, but I knew everything there was to know about what he was doing. We were friends; we shared everything with each other. Well, at least he had shared everything with *me*. I hardly ever said much beyond the superficial. I rarely invited him to my parent's house in Northbrook - where I now lived - nor did I talk with him about matters of the heart. He met a few of my girlfriends and we went out and partied and drank to our heart's delight, but I don't think he ever knew the real me, which was exactly the way I wanted it.

"Jackson Tate, you are the best friend any guy could ever ask for," Nelson had announced to the crowd that gathered at our graduation dinner during the summer of 1992.

I knew he was sincere; it was the kind of person he was. I say 'was' because Nelson had died over six years ago. Cirrhosis of the liver. He seemed to ignore his family history and was rarely found sober while opportunity after opportunity had dried up before him, more than likely because of what I had done years ago. After college he had a few novels published and was a longtime member of the University faculty. His crime fiction had met with moderate success, but nothing to the likes of what he could have achieved had I not become a major roadblock.

I've not slept well since Nelson died, and with each passing year I sleep even less. Sometimes when I lay awake at night I can see shadows crawl into my bedroom, slithering through the tiniest of cracks in my window pane and along my newly painted walls until they morphed into human form and rose high above my bed. They would stare at me, taunting me as if I'm a "person of interest" in some terrorist investigation. A few times I've had awakened as if someone had given me a hard shove, and whenever I turn over and look around I see them again. Standing there. Motionless. Watching me from their deeper realm of darkness. Denying me my ability to sleep. But what I found waiting for me tonight was noticeably different. There was something peculiar about these marauders that had fallen just beyond their usual modus operandi.

There was a fresh shadow among them. It was shorter, stockier. The others had stepped aside while this one took center stage in front of my bed, its penumbra cast against my thirty-seven inch television screen. The shape slowly expanded and contracted and appeared to menace me as I lay under my covers, too afraid to move a single inch.

And as if this were at all possible, the shape seemed to relish in toying with me.

***

1:55 am

The stare down had continued; the inward-outward movements of this stout little shadow against my bedroom wall had me completely spellbound. Stuck. Unsure of what to do next. Once or twice I might have moved, and depending on the direction, the entire group of shadows seemed to shift toward that side of my bed. I was trapped; two shadows to my left, three to my right. And one that sat dead center. Waiting.

For the life of me, I had no idea what they wanted, or if any of this was real at all. I had asked myself this question with each passing night. Was all this a figment of my imagination? Perhaps an outward projection of my own deep-seeded guilt for my treachery? Or maybe it was the result of some chronic form of "twilight paralysis," as my father used to call it, where I was actually half-asleep but aware of my conscious surroundings. On more than one occasion I had thought this could be my answer, that this could simply be my mind playing tricks on me for not falling into the lowest depths of sleep so often. I couldn't tell. Since I haven't held a regular job for many years, I could essentially nap whenever I wanted, for however long I wanted. My agent, editor and friends all knew not to call me between two and five in the afternoon, leaving me at peace to make up for the rest I had lost the previous night. Napping had helped, but my body could never catch up with itself because my sleep cycle was so scattered. I usually wrote from six in the morning until around noon. I would have lunch, take my afternoon *"Rolfy"* (named after a dear friend who was fond of daytime naps), get up in time for dinner and do some editing from the work I had done for the day, then go into my evening routine. Essentially I slept enough to keep me functioning, but never enough to be completely rested, so as a result my nocturnal nemeses would regularly come to visit me.

My lack of sleep had actually cost me my last two relationships, if you can believe that. Around the time my 'friends' began to arrive, I was happily engaged to be married. She was beautiful - everything I had ever wanted - but I had kept her up at night so much that she too had become affected by my lack of sleep. She thought I was going crazy, screaming in the middle of the night, and decided to call it quits before she too became a zombie as I had. Imagine that; leaving your fiancée because of a scorching case of insomnia! In a way, I guess I couldn't blame her. Asking someone to spend the rest of their life with someone who has a sleeping disorder is hazardous to one's health, I suppose. My second attempt at marriage had yielded the same result.

Any second now my Westminster clock would strike two, the fifth night in a row where I'd been awake to hear it.

***

2:27 am

Again something had snapped me out of my brief slumber, but this time it wasn't what I normally would have expected. A bright light shone across my face, followed by a loud chorus that sounded like something from an old Humphrey Bogart film. I rubbed my bleary eyes and noted my television and DVD player were both, words flashed across the screen: *OMBRES EN BAISSE*, a black and white French movie that I had purchased from some strange antique store in Lincoln Park. I told the old guy who ran the place that I liked noir and he recommended this particular film, which I had tried to watch but fell asleep. My remote control was lying next to me on the bed.

"Must've rolled over and turned it on," I mumbled aloud, taking a moment to yawn and stretch. "Oh well, I've got nothing else better to do. *RIGHT GUYS???*"

I know I appeared strange, talking to myself and all, but I was referring to my nighttime visitors who had temporarily departed now that I had some light in my room. This wasn't the first time that I had noticed they would disappear when the lights came on, but with darkness still lurking outside, I knew wherever they went it couldn't be far. In fact, I had no doubt they were still here somewhere, hiding behind the light like a chameleon that changes its colors to blend in. Perhaps they were relieved to be "off-duty" for a while, since they no longer needed to stand guard over me now that my DVD player was about to do their job for a while. Whatever the reason, I didn't care. I just wanted them gone – even if it was only temporary.

I had no idea why I decided to purchase this particular movie; certainly there were other classics under 'film noir' that I could have selected, but I chose this instead. I already have *The Big Sleep*, *Night and the City*, *Cape Fear*, *The Manchurian Candidate* and several others from the Exclusive Edition Collection, so I thought I might give this new film a try. Perhaps it was the late hour or my lack of sleep - or both - but I couldn't remember what the old man who sold it to me had said this movie was about. The DVD sleeve was on my dresser, but it was blank; there was no description at all, except the title *Ombres en Baisse*.

How strange. I've purchased plenty of foreign films over the years, but this was the first time I had received one where there was no summary. I guess I should have paid more attention to the package when I bought it, but that strange old black gentleman had said *'it was something I would never forget'*. In a way, I agreed with him; that would be the last time I bought anything based on some stranger's word.

The title was still on the screen in French. I tried to add subtitles, but the DVD hadn't been formatted for them. Indeed I had bought a *foreign* film, one in which I had no idea what I was watching. Only two names – which I assumed were the actors – had appeared on the screen, neither of which I had recognized. The score for the opening credits was from Berlioz' *Symphonie Fantastique 5: Dream of a Witches' Sabbath*, which I absolutely despised. The droning tuba and the clanging of the bells sounded like a funeral march and had always given me the creeps, so I bypassed the remaining credits until I came to something that looked like action. I climbed into bed and began to watch, hoping once things started moving, I could figure out what was happening so this wouldn't be a total waste of time and money. Until then, I would remain as patient as possible.

***

The film opened inside someone's house, the camera panned through the living room and into the dining room, through the kitchen and made a loop down a long hallway until it came back to the front of the house, pausing at the base of a winding staircase. It began to ascend; at the top of the staircase was a large window with a panoramic view of the sprawling countryside at night, the occasional flash of lightning off in the distance brightened the screen. The camera paused a moment, giving the viewer a full view into the night sky, lightning bolts gave a brief glimpse of several dark clouds that had been invisible in the darkness. The camera backed away from the window and went directly to a ticking grandfather clock just as it announced the hour.

Midnight.

The camera again backed away and went up a second set of stairs, down a long hallway and into the Master Bedroom. Lightning continued to flash and as the camera approached the bed the outline of a man sleeping became clearer. Whoever this was, he was not having a peaceful rest; he turned and tossed until he woke up shouting just as a loud crackle of thunder shook the room. His face perfectly square with the camera, cheeks and forehead twitching, soaked in sweat. He looked around his room, panting. The camera had two jump-cuts to show different corners of the room and for a brief moment one could see shadows from the waving trees make their way through the windows and into his room, spilling across the walls and onto his bed.

The man threw aside the covers and stood before the shadows could touch his body, as if he were avoiding a virus. He backed toward the open doorway, the camera going from him to the bed and back as the shadows from both windows on either side of his room had gathered together, bonding as one, then trickled across the floor and slowly trickled to where he stood. A close-up revealed the whites of the man's eyes growing, his fear increasing with each passing second. The shadow continued making its way, so the man dashed into the hallway and down the staircase, looking behind him but seeing nothing.

At the base of the stairs the man looked up with only the occasional flash through the window illuminating any semblance of light.

No shadow.

The man laughed. " Je dois être fou," he says.

The camera follows him into the living room. All his windows are open, the breeze from a storm blew in his curtains; the damp, musty smell of rain and mist replaced the aroma therapy candles that he'd burned the previous evening. The man decides to shut the windows and adjusts afterward to the sound of silence in his house. The camera notes there is still inclement weather outside, but it is very faint until a second thunderclap, louder than the previous one that woke him, startles him. The man jumps, knocking over a vase. He's thrown off balance and steps on a shard in the darkness.

"Merde!" he says.

The man takes a seat on the couch, turns on the light and pulls a large piece of the shattered vase from his left big toe. He winced and hobbled into the kitchen where he began looking for the extra Band-Aids that he kept in his pantry, and...

***

A series of rapid flashes, followed by a low rumbling had alerted me that a storm was coming. My blinds began to dance from the sudden breeze, followed by more lightning. And just like that, it began to pour outside. I got up and closed the windows and was about to get back into bed when I remembered I'd left my windows open downstairs as well.

Though I preferred cold weather and rainy nights, this *'Chicago Hawk'* was pretty treacherous tonight, so I put on my robe and made my way through my dark house. Every step from my bed to the door seemed to take forever and after I had entered the hallway I found myself looking over my shoulder as if I were checking to see who was following me. One particular moment, just before reaching the stairs, I felt something cold touch my shoulder, causing me to jump and throw my back against the wall. The sensation that I had just been touched shot through every nerve in my body. I was truly frightened and couldn't move for several seconds; the doorway to my room seemed to stretch further and further away until it became a single speck of light way off in the distance until it retreated back, as if the corridor had been stretched like a rubber band. I felt light-headed, so I closed my eyes and took a few deep breaths until the feeling subsided.

I opened my eyes again and everything was where it should be.

Despite the cold, I began sweating profusely; my head and neck were soaked and I could feel perspiration run down my chest and back. Something about this moment had struck me as funny as I felt like a mouse in a maze; cornered and trapped, but determined to make it to the end. All of this 'shadow business' wasn't going to get to me, no matter what.

I wiped my forehead and continued on, making my way down the stairs. 'Storm ghosts' were gracefully blowing through my silk curtains and into my living room; the crisp air passed through me at all sides despite the cover of my full-length, cotton-terry robe. My hardwood floors were cool to the touch; my bare feet began to match the temperature the longer I stood still. I rubbed my shoulders and felt the dampness of my robe, then closed each window. The 'ghosts' were now still, and with the exception of a low rumble outside, the house was finally quiet. But as in my bedroom, shadows had begun to collect just outside my windows and creep across the living room walls, their movements like water streaming over the edge of a bathroom sink and onto the floor. Eventually they began to collect and pool until the mass appeared to take shape and stretch upward in the far corner of my room. The shape resembled the most recent of my night time visitors, the inhaling-exhaling more rapid now than before. A loud thunderclap and bolt of lightning came hit just quick enough for me to clearly see someone wearing a dark suit, standing in that corner with their head down, and as a series of rapid claps and flashes, the shape moved closer to where I stood until finally it within reach and grabbed my arm. I screamed, knocking over a vase that had been given to me as a gift when I gave a lecture at Xioping University in Hong Kong. I yanked away from the thing that grabbed me and stepped on something sharp just as my back had pressed against the wall. The lightning flashed long enough to illuminate my living room. The shape had disappeared.

I hobbled to my easy chair and turned on the light so I could see better. Sure enough, there was a small piece from the broken vase in my toe. Fortunately it was large enough where I could remove it without searching for tweezers, so I clenched my teeth, yanked it out and hobbled down the hall toward my kitchen pantry where I kept a large supply of Band-Aids. There wasn't much blood, so I applied cold water to the cut and successfully wrapped my toe, then went back to the front room to sweep up the mess.

"Fuck, I just *HAD* to..."

I stopped sweeping and ran what just happened through my head: left bedroom, scared of shadows, came downstairs, saw something, loud storm outside, knocked over vase, stepped on something, went to kitchen.

I had just repeated the same movements as the character in the movie I was watching. *The exact same movements.*

That's impossible, I thought. I mulled through the sequence again and again, each time becoming increasingly alarmed, so I dropped the broom and dustpan and went back to my bedroom. The film had the character entering his room. He looked at his television, walking toward it when he heard something and turned to his right. I grabbed my remote and went back until I came to the previous scene. Sure enough, I had made every move, even to the same injured toe.

***

3:28 am

I sat on my bed, still trying to process what had just happened. How was it possible that I could watch a movie - one that I have never heard of and has a single character who fears the night as I do - that can track my movements just minutes *before* I even make them? Even down to minor details like the character's fear of shadows, the raging thunderstorm and knocking over the vase in his living room; how could something like this happen? It felt like I was acting out an episode of the Twilight Zone with Rod Serling being the only thing missing.

Once I'd had enough of reviewing that scene I paused the film after the character's return to his bedroom, the camera being front and center with each window on either side of him, a lightning flash, silk drapes and waving trees frozen in space as if the entire world had stood still. In a way, for me, it had. Like the character, I had returned to my room - a room filled with darkness and shadows and fear and thunder and lightning all rolled into one malevolent scene. Several times I looked at my remote control, too afraid to continue watching the film out of fear that something else would happen to me, that this movie would predict what would happen next and that I might not like the end result. One part of me wanted to think like my mother - a woman who had never succumbed to fear and was braver than any person I had ever known - and shake off this moment, classifying it as a mere coincidence. The other half of me, my father's half, said to be smart and stop watching it immediately, take it downstairs and destroy it before something else "coincidental" happens.

I wanted to do that. I wanted to say no to this odd feature, suggested to me by some old black man who owned a crazy store on the west side of town. I remember how he looked at me just before he made his recommendation; the fact that he closed his eyes and continued to breathe deep as if he were somehow taking a whiff of me. He seemed suspicious at first, but once he finished with his 'breathing exercises' and opened his eyes he seemed as right as rain. Accommodating. Genial. It was almost as he had discovered something about me and had made the only suggestion that made sense. But the question is why? Why had this man suggested I watch a French film with no subtitles that appeared to almost predict my future? Was he trying to tell me something? Perhaps I needed to see what was going on so I could decide on my own whether I should alter my next move?

Suddenly the 'mother' side of me had taken over. I grabbed my remote, hit play and started to watch the movie again...

***

The camera followed the man's point of view up the stairs and down the hall. There was a bright light and an indistinguishable sound coming from his bedroom. The point of view shifted to the man's feet, visible against the hardwood floor and showing the band-aid on his left big toe, a creaking sound matched each step.

Now inside the master bedroom, the camera picks up the man as he enters and shifts from right to left as he approaches his bed, still looking for the shadow that seemed to follow him, then focusing on his television set. He strains while looking at the TV, as if to ask the question 'how did this come on', and before he can turn it off he hears a noise and his head snaps quickly to the right.

The camera moves from left to right, following the man as he heads toward a darkened doorway that leads to the master bathroom. The scene cuts to the man as he enters and attempts to turn on the light.

No luck.

He retreats to the bedroom; the camera catches a beam of light that comes toward the dark room once again, the man plays his flashlight across the tiled floor. A toothbrush, paste, nail clippers, a bar of soap and small box of Kleenex lay scattered near the tub suggesting they had been brushed off the bathroom sink.

The man picks up each item from the floor and puts them blindly onto the sink as the bathroom door swings shut behind him, leaving him in complete darkness except for the flashlight, which moves around wildly while sounds of the man struggling with the door can be heard.

"Il y a quelqu'un? Déverrouillez la porte de droite maintenant!"

The beam from the flashlight moves back and forth between the doorknob and the keyhole until the knob begins to turn.

"Qui est là?"

The doorknob stops moving, a roll of thunder and lightning flash through the lone, beveled window in the bathroom, revealing something on the mirror. Just as the man flashes his light on the mirror there are three knocks on his door.

"Qui est là?"

Thunder and lightning hit again, this time the duration is longer. The camera picks up something just as the lights go out again. The man flashes his light across the mirror, words written in either mud or blood - difficult to tell since it was in black and white: "Ombres en Baisse."

"Ombres en Baisse?" I ask, clueless since I know not a speck of French.

The camera focuses on the man's face, a silhouette from below his chin given the flashlight. His face and lips quiver in fear as three loud pounds, followed by a a deep, groaning voice: "Fraaaaaancois! Fraaaaaancois!"

There's more pounding; louder and deeper until the sound of cracking wood fills the air, the camera moves from Francois face until it meets his beam of light, shining on the part of the door that appears on the verge of breaking free. A few more heavy thuds hit the door until finally a fist pushes through...

***

A crashing sound came from my bathroom. I took a quick glance at my TV, the hand now reaching wildly around as Francois continues to scream. 'This won't happen to me', I thought as I searched for my flashlight in my nightstand drawer. I hit the light and approached the doorway with caution, taking one last look around the room. I was even paranoid enough to lock the bedroom door and search my walk-in closet as a precaution.

That task now complete, I continued with my mission, playing my flashlight across the sink, the toilet and onto the floor. Toothpaste, toothbrush, comb, one bar of soap, plastic drinking up and my razor, plus the plastic shelf they all had rested on were all scattered across the floor. Keeping my eye firm on the spilled toiletries I reached for the switch, which came on. There was nothing on the mirror. I turned around, nothing behind me.

I had been wrong. All of this was one strange coincidence that had nothing to do with any movie. I laughed out loud, thinking my problems stemmed from lack of sleep rather than a few strange shadows and an overactive imagination. For much of my adult life, I've tried to avoid taking a sedative to help me sleep, and now that I think about it, my father had problems getting adequate rest. Sleep apnea, my mother told me, once the term had become popular. In his later years - all the way until his death, in fact - he slept with one of those breathing machines and said he had never felt better in his life, so naturally you can understand that Mom and I found it quite ironic that he died sometime in the middle of the night in December of 1994. Heart attack, the coroner said. Catching up on years of sleepless nights, I say.

Perhaps that's why I'm so adverse to taking sedatives or trying one of those funny looking breathing contraptions. I'm afraid that I might be just like dad; years with no decent rest and then I die. Most would probably argue that passing on while unconscious is a gift. In my case, it was my biggest fear.

I turned on the light and bent down to retrieve the falling items; first the shelf, which I mounted back on the wall, then the toothpaste and brush and other items until everything was back as it was. I took a moment to look at myself in the mirror, then ran some cold water and splashed my face, feeling alert and ready to continue this odd film. *Perhaps I should consider a sedative*, I thought. *It surely would help so...*

The door suddenly snapped shut, smashing into the door frame so tight that it cracked the molding around the entrance. The lights went out, and before I could make sense of anything there were three heavy knocks at the door: *Thump! Thump! Thump!*

"Jaaaaacksooooonnnnn! Jaaaaacksoooooonnnn!"

THUMP! THUMP! THUMP!

"JAAAAAAACKSOOOOOONNNN!"

Hearing whatever was outside grumble my name shook me to the core.

"Who's there? What do you want?"

THUMP! THUMP! THUMP!

"JAAAAAAACKSOOOOOONNNN!"

"Who's there?" I asked again, playing my flashlight along the door until I heard the doorknob squeaking with each turn, followed by a series of loud thuds.

"WHO'S THERE?" I shouted, just as a fist had punched a hole through the door, a gangly arm forced its way through all the way up to the elbow, fingers reaching out in a blind attempt to grasp whatever it could.

My feet were nailed to the floor; even if I wanted to move I knew I couldn't put one foot in front of the other, so the only thing I could do was cover my eyes like a coward. Nelson used to do that very same thing whenever we watched horror films in our dorm room on campus. Once we had our girlfriends over on Halloween night and watched a triple feature: *Halloween*, *The Exorcist* and *He Knows You're Alone*, the film that actually was Tom Hanks' first movie. Me, Michelle and Natasha had a blast, but Nelson appeared somewhat terrified for much of the night. He had covered his eyes more times than the girls had, so much so that I couldn't resist the temptation to scare him from behind, using the light from the television to appear as some grotesque beast crawling out of the shadows. I never realized exactly how frightened Nelson had been of the dark until then, for I scared him so bad he actually pissed himself and ran into our bathroom, completely embarrassed. Michelle never saw him again after that night. Now that I think of it, that Halloween of 1993 was the beginning of the end of our friendship. Nelson loved that girl and all she did from that point on was laugh at him, both to his face and behind his back. His drinking was out of control and I can rarely recall a moment when he was sober again.

Funny how I was now the one covering their eyes, every bit as afraid as my deceased friend had once been. Maybe even worse.

The room outside my closed eyes had grown quiet; no more pounding or breaking wood or scratching around, so I uncovered my eyes and looked around. My door was wide open. There was no hole in it. No splintered wood on the floor. And most importantly, there was no one standing there, waiting for me. I began to wonder again if this was my imagination running wild, perhaps a guilty conscience for my past transgressions that had finally come to roost. Suddenly I began to *feel* how tired I was; the last remnants of adrenaline from my perceived circumstance had ebbed away leaving me barely able to stand, to comprehend whether any of this was actually happening. I could finally walk again and took one careful step after another, my heart feeling as if it were on the verge of bursting through my chest. As I entered my bedroom it seemed as if the trees from outside had sensed my presence and began to shake from the storm outside, shadows played through the window and across my walls, some long enough to creep on my hardwood floor until I was so paranoid that I stepped out of their way to avoid contact. I came face to face with my flat-screen, noting that Francois was doing the exact same thing as I was.

Standing and staring...

***

The camera held Francois' face front and center in the screen, his eyes darting back and forth as if he were in a mad panic. A trickle of sweat dripped down his forehead and into his left eye, causing him to blink several times, though he never took a moment to dry it. The camera flashed between his face and television several times, each time coming closer until it was clear that Francois was watching himself look at himself on the screen. He seemed on the verge of a nervous breakdown, grabbing his hair and babbling something aloud as he back away from the screen as a deep darkness began to fall all around him. The television showed Francois' backward motion and shadows falling all around him. The camera flickered twice, then suddenly there appeared a black, oval-shaped mass that appeared on screen that hovered slowly toward Francois. The camera jumped to Francois, then back to the TV screen. To Francois, the screen. It repeated these quick series of jump cuts until Francois let out a blood-curdling scream and the screen went pitch black...

***

3:59 am

The crackle of thunder sent shivers through me, like cold water that filled each vein throughout my body. My TV went dark as if someone had pulled the plug; the marauders that were once my nighttime companions had returned, all except for one - the shortest of the group. They crept into my bedroom through each window and surrounded me, their shapes becoming more defined as they came closer. I had been pressed into the center of my room, my back to the flat-screen TV that had shown the strangest film I had even seen. What did these figures want of me? Why now? There must be something I'm missing here, and...

A light flashed from behind...the TV! I turned and, just like Francois, I could see my own image in the screen as if a camera were suspended on the wall behind me. I could also see the five shadows standing around me; motionless, heads down as they had been every night for as long as I could remember. I looked to my left and right; sure enough, there they were. I took a step toward the door, but there was a shadow in my way, and noting my sudden move it grew and stretched into the size of a defensive lineman, inhaling and exhaling as the missing shadow had earlier. I took a step back, the shadow shrunk back to it's "normal" size just as the screen began to flicker and contort, the color slowly bleached out until it resembled the black and white film I had just watched. I could see each shadow raise their head and extend their arm toward the TV, their fingers growing until they formed a shape that was now visible in my television. The mass had blacked-out the light, then two large eyes had opened and a left hand followed by a right reached out into the air and slammed onto my hardwood floor. The eyes remained nice and big on my screen until whatever held onto my floor had strained hard enough until I could see a head, then shoulders, then legs, then feet fall into my room.

The sixth shadow had crawled out of my television, stood and opened its eyes. Though I could make out where shoulders and a neck and head should be, everything kept moving and shifting like a jellyfish swimming in the ocean. Each step toward me was the equivalent of two in 'real time'. I don't remember what happened for those few seconds, but when my senses had returned I was on the floor, looking at the original five loom over me. I picked up my head and saw 'number six' on its hands and knees, eyes opened, crawling toward me like a panther in the darkness. I tried to scream, but nothing came out of me as a rapid fire of lightning and thunder hit, brightening up the room. Standing around me were the ghosts of my favorite writers, now deceased: Edgar Allen Poe, H. P. Lovecraft, Agatha Christie, Bram Stoker and Montague Rhodes-James. And now - hovering over me, eyes boring directly into my forehead - was one writer whom I knew all too well. One whose life and work and ideas that I had stolen and used as my own and forged into a lengthy career all for myself.

His name was *Nelson Ade.*

Nelson's blank stare told me everything that I needed to know, what it was that he wanted from me, and as he continued his assault - his face coming closer, each fraction of a second seeming like an eternity - I closed my own eyes for the very last time, content that he must have his justice and that I must pay for my acts of perdition.

***

18 Hours Later

My breathing is deeper than ever before. My body is flexible, contorted, spindly. Of course I could never have felt this way being human, but now my entire existence has been reduced to darkness, to the world of the 'real and un-real', to the depths of man's fears and the valley of their insecurities. I have become the thing that goes bump in the night, the cause of the hair that stands on the back of people's necks, the being that lurks in people's periphery vision, then suddenly disappears. I am now The Shadow. I prey upon the weak of mind and heart, the guilty, the sinful, the reckless, the one who lives at the expense of others and is afraid of their own payback. I am a reminder of the tyranny of evil men and the one who is always one step behind those who think they have successfully evaded their payback.

I am what is done in darkness before it comes to the light.

But what I have noticed in the short time allowed to roam freely in dark corners and long hallways is that only those who fear me, who have something they wish to hide from rest of the world, can sense my presence. Only *them* can I put in their place, as I have learned in my brief tenure. I have stood here for two hours, watching myself in the middle of a perfect slumber, hoping to enact some sort of revenge upon Nelson for taking my soul and exchanging it for his. He has figured out a way to take my body for himself, a second chance at life where he can go back to work - healthy, alive and probably with more stories to tell than ever before. He had once lived as I now do; seeing the other side of life - the *unlife* - and has now returned to write all about it. Though limited, I could see him through the smallest of cracks in closets and cupboards during the day, working away to his heart's content, finishing four short stories in a single day and brimming with ideas to work on for tomorrow. That was the old Nelson, or shall I say the new 'Jackson', that I've always known. And now, through a complete stroke of good luck - or in my case, bad luck -

he had found a way to come back and live the life of a writer that he always desired and deserved. He had written a masterpiece; a novella that had been discovered sitting alone on a shelf in a small bookstore in Paris, France. A story that he had written after he discovered what I had done; a story that he had written and self-published in French, a language that he both loved and knew I had never studied. Nelson had self-published it and managed to sell it many years ago to an overseas distributor who loved American Horror and put it on shelves near the University of Paris, where a film student happened to read it and adapted it into a short feature that won him a prize for Best Foreign Short Noir at the North American Film Festival in Chicago six years ago. I didn't know any of this when that old black man sold me this DVD in that strange store of his, called The Dhamira Curio and Gift Shop over on the west side. But I do now. I know all of this as I sit and observe Nelson, now camouflaged as me, in my bed sleeping peacefully for the first time since his death six years ago. I even know the name of his book, both in French and English. That's the benefit of being a 'Shadow', you have the gift of being aware of any and everything related to those whom you follow in the darkness. I didn't have this knowledge before, but I certainly do now.

The name of this feature, you ask? That's easy: *Ombres en Baisse*, which in English translates to *Shadows Fall*.

Rather fitting, don't you think?

David T. Boyd

2: *the obituaries*

THE CHICAGO DAILY READER

(Obituaries: December 29, 1974)

Mr. Thomas Gannon, owner of the Dhamira Curio and Gift Shop, located in the Bronzeville neighborhood on Chicago's South Side, died on December 25, 1974. Mr. Gannon was born to Herman and Beulah (Holton) Gannon on October 19, 1934 in Little Rock, Arkansas. "He was a wonderful, generous friend who had helped very many people," explained friend and assistant store manager James Masterson. "He was gracious with customers, many of whom became his friends. He shared his friends with me and they are now my friends."

Mr. Gannon's parents moved to Chicago during the summer of 1938, where he grew up in Bronzeville. He attended Jean Baptiste Ponte DuSable High School, where he graduated in 1952 at the top of his class. He went to The University of Chicago and obtained a Bachelor's Degree in history, minoring in archeological studies, and became one of very few black men allowed to take part in digs in Portuguese East Africa (now Mozambique), Kenya and Tanzania, which he did for twelve years. He returned to Chicago in 1968 and shortly thereafter met his future wife, Cynthia. They had one son, Michael.

While in Africa, Mr. Gannon learned Swahili and brought back with him several artifacts discovered during his many digs. He also became intrigued in African Folklore and ensconced himself in the history of legendary tribal beliefs, including the thought that everything was alive and could potentially reflect the conscience of those with whom it comes into contact. Regarding this last comment, Mr. Gannon once said: *"if we come to understand that everything has a soul, a conscience, then mankind would strive to respect ALL aspects of life, not merely that which concerns us."*

Mr. Gannon's father passed away during his tenure in Africa and subsequently left behind a small inheritance that allowed him to open the *Dhamira Curio and Gift Shop* in Bronzeville, where customers were intrigued by odd artifacts and rarely seen gifts, as well as common party favors and balloons, particularly "smiley-face" balloons. Those who frequented his store said it had a different feel to it, one rarely seen by black-owned businesses of his time.

"The place was definitely intriguing and had a character all its own. Some days I would walk in and feel as if the entire store was alive and bursting with stories," said Beverly Thomas, longtime Bronzeville resident. "Mr. Gannon was always easy-going and polite. And since he was from the neighborhood, that meant a lot to all of us."

Mr. Gannon moved into a two-story bungalow on Wabash Avenue, where he lived with his wife and son until his untimely death.

THE CROSSTOWN HERALD

(Obituaries: December 28, 1974)

Mr. Thomas M. Gannon, a resident of Bronzeville, sadly passed away in his home on Christmas Day. He was known as a "very friendly and approachable man" who loved his friends and family, was very active in community events and well-read in a variety of subjects.

Mr. Gannon, a graduate of The University of Chicago, was noted for his travels. He spent twelve years in Africa on numerous archeological digs and kept very detailed notes of his experiences, which later became a memoir, titled *From the Desert to the City*, published in 1971 (The University of Chicago Press). Chicago Tribune literary reviewer Felix Lazlo had this to say about his work: *"Tom Gannon's memoir is a marvelous kaleidoscope of fact, exploration, struggle and victory. His book is not only about the noted findings of a celebrated archaeologist, but is a careful examination of the soul of man juxtaposed with the discovery of lost artifacts in human history. A triumph!"*

With money saved from an inheritance, Mr. Gannon opened the Dhamira Curio and Gift Shop in Bronzeville, which he owned and managed until his untimely death. He is survived by his wife Cynthia and son Michael.

David T. Boyd

3: *the tributes*

(From Thomas Gannon's homegoing service
held Saturday, December 28, 1974)

Dear Tommy

By Cassaundra Hutchinson-Taylor

Tommy and I grew up together in Bronzeville. I'm not sure, but I think I was his very first friend, and since he never argued with me after the million or so times I would mention it in front of people, I suppose he agreed with me. He was always decent like that, and even if I wasn't the first, he made me feel I was and would never contradict me. That's the kind of guy he was.

I remember meeting him at Crispus Attucks Preschool. From my recollection, he had just moved to Chicago from Little Rock, Arkansas and had been here all of a week when he came to class. He dressed like he was from the south, too - whatever that means. Kind of like *Pig Pen* from Peanuts, minus the cloud of dust: overalls, white shirt and socks, Converse All-Star gym shoes. His hair was neatly combed and parted. He was real prim and proper and had a thick southern drawl and would open doors for people, especially the other girls in our class. Tommy wasn't like other kids our age; not like that, anyway. He was just himself at all times, and the rest of us took notice. He was smart and funny - in a droll sort of way - and athletic and a people magnet. The most interesting part was he never forced himself on anyone. By just being *Tommy* he attracted plenty of attention, even though it wasn't his intention. That was the cool thing about him. But what really spoke volumes was his ability to remain balanced. He never let his gift of being a people-person get in the way of being decent. He was like that in pre-school, grammar school, high school and college. I had never seen anyone overachieve so easily. It really was quite remarkable to watch.

When we were seniors at DuSable, I remember how honored I was when he asked me to the prom. At that time he was the B.M.O.C, being a football star and all. He talked to a lot of girls, but never dated anyone for very long. Every girl at school wondered who he was going to ask to the dance, and since they knew we were friends, they figured I had the inside scoop. Honestly, I didn't know a thing, and that's what I told the other girls. Little did Tommy know, but I got so many requests that eventually I started "charging" people to put in a good word for them. I made almost ten dollars in a week, and had more requests until I made a general announcement to everyone about his status. To my surprise, Tommy actually asked me to go to the prom. When I asked him 'why me', he said it was because I was the only one who didn't ask. (*She laughs*) Look, I secretly loved him, though I tried to act like I didn't. And since we were such close friends I was always afraid that dating would ruin what we already had. I know - strange, right? But that's why I never approached him. I was glad he did.

After high school we continued to date. He went to University of Chicago and I went to University of Illinois - Chicago Circle, as it was called back then. We kept dating and he became deeply rooted in history and was starting to go across the country on archaeological digs, primarily in New Mexico and Arizona. Around then he started talking about going to India and Africa once he graduated, but he knew I wasn't interested in going with him. I felt bad. I felt as if I were holding him up, and I could tell he was trying to do things that made me happy instead of being true to himself. Then came the day he asked me to marry him. I turned him down. I knew I had broken his heart, and mine was broken as well, but how could I possibly stay in the way of his dreams? He knew good and well I didn't want to go to Africa. Too much heat and bugs and stuff for a girl like me, you know? But that was all he talked about, see? And if we had gotten married, I wouldn't have been able to forgive myself for not letting him go. I was devastated, but held firm despite my feelings, though I escorted him to the airport the day he left. (*Cassaundra pauses to regain her composure*) Neither of us cried, but I practically drowned myself in tears back in the parking lot. I'm sure he cried too at some point.

We exchanged letters for quite a while and saw each other when he returned to Chicago once every year or so. Admittedly, I held onto the thought of us being together when he decided to come back; that is until I met my beautiful husband Heathcliff during the summer of 1964. The tone of our letters had noticeably changed - when I actually *sent* them, that is. Tommy had less and less to say, until one day he asked me if I were withholding something from him. That's when I finally told him about Cliff, that we were engaged and hoped to be married soon. For a long while there was no communication between the two of us, until one day I received a short note written in Swahili that said: *Asiye kuwapo na lake halipo.* Of course, I had no idea what that meant, so I went to see a friend at Chicago State University whom I knew had studied Swahili. She read this and smiled, saying: *"If you are absent you lose your share."* It figures that Tommy would say that, both in the language and in general. Like me, he knew that was the chance he took by leaving. I was glad to finally hear him express that.

From that moment on, I knew things were well between us again. We had found a way to salvage the love we felt for one another, and Tommy couldn't have been happier for Cliff and me. He ordered roses for us that we received on the day of our wedding and sent some artifacts from Africa as gifts that we still have on the shelf in our front room. Some might think I should have gone with him, but I disagree. Had it not been for him, I wouldn't have met my Cliff, nor would I have been ready and open to finding such a wonderful man. (*She smiles, while glancing at her husband*) In the end, everything worked out for the best and there's nothing I would change. Tommy helped me find my sanctuary; isn't that what real friends are supposed to do?

So, dear Tommy, now that I'm in your presence for the last time, I just simply want to thank you for being such a great friend to all of us. We were so blessed to have you for so long, and though we'll miss you terribly, we know you are watching over us from a distance.

My Friend, My Brother

By Roger Dunwoodie

Good morning everyone. I'm Roger Dunwoodie, and I had the pleasure of having Tom Gannon as my best friend for over twenty years. Tommy was a real good guy; very smart and kind, always had something inspirational to say and never failed to share himself to those around him, regardless if they were a friend or stranger. In fact, for almost the entire time we had known one another, I hardly recall seeing him angry. Tommy just wasn't that kind of person. He had a certain charisma that could light up a room, even when that room appeared to be hostile toward him for no good reason. He was calm and collected, but very tough and he refused to take any crap from anyone. I knew that from the very beginning.

I'd met him during my first semester at the University of Chicago, where we shared a dorm room together. I remember the resident assistant came to "warn" me that some black person (and that's not the word he used) would be my roommate for the semester and if I wanted to switch he would speak to the housing director. I grew up in Bridgeport, so needless to say I had never been around any black people for any length of time. Occasionally I saw a few on the bus or the train, but I'd never had any as friends. My father was very bigoted, and once used to boast about his involvement in the Bridgeport Riots, but it ultimately was my mother who was the buffer, often saying "do unto others as they did unto you." I truly felt she meant that, even though I hardly remember her talking directly to blacks, other than in stores or on trains. Regardless, it didn't matter to me, and I told the RA of my floor that I wouldn't mind having him as my roommate. To this day, I'm glad I did.

Tommy and I became fast friends. At first, no one would speak to him on our floor and there were a few jerks around who tried to give him some trouble, but within a few months he became one of the most popular guys in our dorm. He always looked people in the eye and carried himself with such elegance and class that you had no choice but to either like him or get out of his way. He was well-read and thought quickly on his feet, so it was hard for people to pull the wool over his eyes. But one of the greatest things about Tommy was his offbeat sense of humor, and if he knew you well enough, he would tell the most off-the-wall jokes ever that would go right over your head if you weren't careful. One day, during our second year at University of Chicago, Tommy and I were studying for a chemistry exam in the library when he whispered: *"Hey Rog, what did the Hollywood director say to the young neuron who wanted to become a movie star?"* I said *"I dunno"*, and without missing a beat, he looked right at me and said: *"Hey kid, you've got real potential."* (Roger pauses, laughs) At first I didn't get it, then once it hit me I kept snickering until this very old librarian wearing scorpion glasses and a black shawl threatened to kick me out if I didn't pipe down.

Another time he and I went to this soul food place called Army and Lou's over on East 75th Street, near South Park Way (now King Drive). Tommy had been talking about this place for almost as long as we'd known each other, so I decided to try it. I was the only white guy in the place, but that didn't stop him from being himself. He knew everybody in the place, including the owner, who came over and greeted us. The man was very pleasant and tried making a few recommendations, thinking that I had never heard of ham hocks and black-eyed peas before. Little did he know that Tommy's parents had brought over several trays of soul food to our dorm room, so I felt at home with the menu and already knew what I wanted. Now I'll say this: the better you get to know me, the more you'll find that I'm kind of a "quirky" guy. Tommy already figured that out about me, so as we waited for our meal, I remember telling Tommy *"sometimes I eat my whole meal using my salad fork."* I knew that would mess with him, and since I was always on the receiving end of his jokes, I thought I'd get a little revenge. But, as I said before, he was a real smart guy. He didn't say a word for a long time, and I could tell he was trying to think of a response. I always knew when he was ready to reply because his face would lose all expression. Once our food had arrived, he picked up his salad fork and examined it for almost a minute, then said: *"I have to ask you something, Rog. By eating your ENTIRE meal with a salad fork does that include the soup?"* (*Roger laughs again, as does the audience*).

Both of us graduated from U of C in '56. Tommy went off to Africa while I stayed behind and went to law school. I tried to convince him to become a lawyer, saying we'd make a great team someday if we ever decided to go into business together. I thought he had a great mind for that kind of work, but it was clear his real passion was to go on all these exotic digs, which I had no patience for whatsoever. But despite the distance, I would hear from him regularly by mail, and whenever he was in town we would always get together for dinner or a Bears game or something and have a great time. I truly miss...(*Roger pauses, eyes tearing, clears throat*)...excuse me...I truly miss the many good times we had together and I'm sorry I won't ever have the chance to see him again (*long pause*). His passing was far too sudden for such a wonderful person, but I know I can't sit around feeling sorry for myself because Tommy just wouldn't have that sort of thing. Definitely not from me. So I guess I'd better get off my duff and keep moving forward because he'd have it no other way.

You know, I'm so grateful to my mother for a lot of things. As you can see by looking at me, she was a good cook. She showed me how to dress properly, keep myself groomed and polished for all occasions. But the most important lesson she ever taught me was acceptance; acceptance of people for who they were rather than what they looked like or what part of town they came from. Without this very basic, but imperative, lesson shared with me by my beautiful mother, I might never have met such a special person who shared himself with me so freely. He was a beautiful human being and my world became a bit sadder now that he's gone. (*Roger takes a long pause, eventually regains his composure*).

Thank you for everything, Tommy. You were my friend, my brother.

David T. Boyd was born and raised in Chicago, Illinois, but now lives in Brooklyn, New York. The Dhamira Curio and Gift Shop Volume One is his fifth release. Mr. Boyd graduated from St. Ignatius College Preparatory in Chicago, received his Bachelor of Arts in English from SUNY Empire State College and a Master of Fine Arts in Creative Writing from The City College of New York. Besides writing, Mr. Boyd loves to exercise, discuss politics and tell everyone why Chicago is the center of the universe. His four previous books - *Falling Down, Mystery, Malevolence & Murder Volume One, Sammy's Carol and Mystery, Malevolence & Murder Volume Two* - are available through Amazon, Barnes & Noble, as well as his official website, www.davidtboyd.com.

www.ingramcontent.com/pod-product-compliance
Lightning Source LLC
Chambersburg PA
CBHW030633130626
46552CB00002B/837